"I should have just slept with him," she murmured, the declaration sounding unbearably loud in the silent house.

Then at least she'd have a good reason to regret her actions.

"It's not too late to change your mind," a low male voice said from the doorway.

Startled, Hadley whirled in Liam's direction. Heat seared her cheeks. "I thought you went out."

"I did, but it wasn't any fun without you." He advanced toward her, his intent all too clear.

When his arms went around her, pulling her tight against his strong body, Hadley stopped resisting. This was what she wanted. Why fight against something that felt this right?

"Kiss me quick before I change my mind," she told him, her head falling back so she could meet his gaze. "And don't stop."

* * *

Nanny Makes Three is part of the series
Texas Cattleman's Club:
Lies and Lullabies—Baby secrets and a
scheming sheikh rock Royal, Texas.

Dear Reader,

I am always grateful to have the opportunity to participate in a Texas Cattleman's Club continuity and returning to Royal, Texas, was great fun. My hero, Liam Wade, is a horse rancher and I really enjoyed all the videos I watched on reining, barrel racing and cutting horses. It's pretty amazing what these horses and riders achieve by working together.

If my hero was going to be a world-class reining horse trainer and competitor, he needed a woman who matched him in talent and daring. Hadley Stratton, barrel racer turned nanny, must come to terms with the mistakes she made in the past if she's going to have a chance at happiness. Luckily she has a determined man to help her.

I hope you enjoy Liam and Hadley's story.

All the best,

Cat Schield

NANNY MAKES THREE

—

CAT SCHIELD

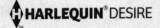
HARLEQUIN® DESIRE

Special thanks and acknowledgment are given
to Cat Schield for her contribution to the
Texas Cattleman's Club: Lies and Lullabies miniseries.

ISBN-13: 978-0-373-73433-7

Nanny Makes Three

Copyright © 2016 by Harlequin Books S.A.

Recycling programs
for this product may
not exist in your area.

This is a work of fiction. Names, characters, places and incidents are
either the product of the author's imagination or are used fictitiously,
and any resemblance to actual persons, living or dead, business
establishments, events or locales is entirely coincidental.

This edition published by arrangement with Harlequin Books S.A.

For questions and comments about the quality of this book,
please contact us at CustomerService@Harlequin.com.

Printed in U.S.A.

Cat Schield has been reading and writing romance since high school. Although she graduated from college with a BA in business, her idea of a perfect career was writing books for Harlequin. And now, after winning the Romance Writers of America 2010 Golden Heart® Award for series contemporary romance, that dream has come true. Cat lives in Minnesota with her daughter, Emily, and their Burmese cat. When she's not writing sexy, romantic stories for Harlequin Desire, she can be found sailing with friends on the St. Croix River, or in more exotic locales, like the Caribbean and Europe. She loves to hear from readers. Find her at catschield.com. Follow her on Twitter: @catschield.

Books by Cat Schield

Harlequin Desire

The Sherdana Royals

Royal Heirs Required
A Royal Baby Surprise

Las Vegas Nights

At Odds with the Heiress
A Merger by Marriage
A Taste of Temptation

Texas Cattleman's Club: Lies and Lullabies

Nanny Makes Three

Visit her Author Profile page
at Harlequin.com, or
catschield.com, for more titles.

For Jeff and Roxanne Schall of Shada Arabians

One

Shortly after the 6:00 a.m. feeding, Liam Wade strode through the barn housing the yearling colts and fillies, enjoying the peaceful crunching of hay and the occasional equine snort. It was January 1, and because of the way horses were classified for racing and showing purposes, regardless of their calendar age, every horse in every stall on the ranch was now officially a year older.

Dawn of New Year's Day had never been a time of reflection for Liam. Usually he was facedown in a beautiful woman's bed, sleeping like the dead after an evening of partying and great sex. Last year that had changed. He'd left the New Year's Eve party alone.

His cell phone buzzed in his back pocket, and he pulled it out. The message from his housekeeper made him frown.

There's a woman at the house who needs to speak to you.

Liam couldn't imagine what sort of trouble had come knocking on his door this morning. He texted back that he was on his way and retraced his steps to his Range Rover.

As he drove up, he saw an unfamiliar gray Ford Fusion in the driveway near the large Victorian house Liam's great-great-grandfather had built during the last days of the nineteenth century. Liam and his twin brother, Kyle, had grown up in this seven-bedroom home, raised by their grandfather after their mother headed to Dallas to create her real estate empire.

Liam parked and turned off the engine. A sense of foreboding raised the hair on his arms, and he wondered at his reluctance to get out of the truck. He'd enjoyed how peaceful the last year had been. A strange woman showing up at the crack of dawn could only mean trouble.

Slipping from behind the wheel, Liam trotted across the drought-dry lawn and up the five steps that led to the wraparound porch. The stained glass windows set into the double doors allowed light to filter into the wide entry hall, but prevented him from seeing inside. Thus, it wasn't until Liam pushed open the door that he saw the infant car seat off to one side of the hall. As that was registering, a baby began to wail from the direction of the living room.

The tableau awaiting him in the high-ceilinged room was definitely the last thing he'd expected. Candace, his housekeeper, held a squalling infant and was obviously trying to block the departure of a stylish woman in her late fifties.

"Liam will be here any second," Candace was saying. With her focus split between the child and the blonde woman in the plum wool coat, his housekeeper hadn't noticed his arrival.

"What's going on?" Liam questioned, raising his voice slightly to be heard above the unhappy baby.

The relief on Candace's face was clear. "This is Diane Garner. She's here about her granddaughter."

"You're Liam Wade?" the woman demanded, her tone an accusation.

"Yes." Liam was completely bewildered by her hostility. He didn't recognize her name or her face.

"My daughter is dead."

"I'm very sorry to hear that."

"She was on her way to see you when she went into

labor and lost control of her car. The doctors were unable to save her."

"That's very tragic." Liam wasn't sure what else to say. The name Garner rang no bells. "Did she and I have an appointment about something?"

Diane stiffened. "An appointment?"

"What was your daughter's name?"

"Margaret Garner. You met her in San Antonio." Diane grew more agitated with each word she uttered. "You can't expect me to believe you don't remember."

"I'm sorry," Liam said, pitching his voice to calm the woman. She reminded him of a high-strung mare. "It's been a while since I've been there."

"It's been eight months," Diane said. "Surely you couldn't have forgotten my daughter in such a short period of time."

Liam opened his mouth to explain that he wasn't anywhere near San Antonio eight months ago when it hit him what the woman was implying. He turned and stared at the baby Candace held.

"You think the baby's mine?"

"Her name is Maggie and I know she's yours."

Liam almost laughed. This was one child he knew without question wasn't his. He'd been celibate since last New Year's Eve. "I assure you that's not true."

Diane pursed her lips. "I came here thinking you'd do the right thing by Maggie. She's your child. There's no question that you had an affair with my daughter."

He wasn't proud of the fact that during his twenties, he'd probably slept with a few women without knowing their last name or much more about them other than that they were sexy and willing. But he'd been careful, and not one of them had shown up on his doorstep pregnant.

"If I had an affair with your daughter, it was a long time ago, and this child is not mine."

"I have pictures that prove otherwise." Diane pulled a

phone out of her purse and swiped at the screen. "These are you and my daughter. The date stamp puts them at eight months ago in San Antonio. Are you going to deny that's you?"

The screen showed a very pretty woman with blond hair and bright blue eyes, laughing as she kissed the cheek of a very familiar-looking face. Kyle's. A baseball cap hid his short hair, but the lack of a scar on his chin left no doubt it was Kyle and not Liam in the picture.

"I realize that looks like me, but I have a twin brother." Liam was still grappling with seeing his brother looking so happy when Diane Garner slipped past him and headed toward the entry. "But even so, that doesn't mean the baby is a Wade."

Diane paused with her hand on the front doorknob. Her eyes blazed. "Margaret dated very infrequently, and she certainly didn't sleep around. I can tell from the pictures that she really fell for you."

Either Diane hadn't heard Liam when he explained that he had a twin or she saw this as an excuse. While he grappled for a way to get through to the woman, she yanked the door open and exited the house.

Stunned, Liam stared after her. He was ready to concede that the child might be a Wade. A DNA test would confirm that quickly enough, but then what? Kyle was on active duty in the military and not in a position to take on the responsibility of an infant.

The baby's cries escalated, interrupting his train of thought. He turned to where Candace rocked the baby in an effort to calm her and realized Diane Garner intended to leave her granddaughter behind. Liam chased after the older woman and caught her car door before she could close it.

"Are you leaving the baby?"

"Margaret was on her way to see you. I think she meant

to either give you Maggie or get your permission to give
her up. There were blank forms to that effect in her car."

"Why?"

"She never wanted to have children of her own." Diane's voice shook. "And I know she wouldn't have been
able to raise one by herself."

"What happens if I refuse?"

"I'll turn her over to child services."

"But you're the child's grandmother. Couldn't you just
take care of her until we can get a DNA test performed
and…"

"Because of health issues, I'm not in a position to take
care of her. You're Maggie's father," Diane insisted. "She
belongs with you."

She belonged with her father. Unfortunately, with Kyle
on active duty, could he care for a baby? Did he even want
to? Liam had no idea—it had been two years since he'd
last spoken with Kyle. But if the child was a Wade—and
Liam wasn't going to turn the child out until he knew one
way or another—that meant she belonged here.

"How do I get in contact with you?" Liam asked. Surely
the woman would want some news of her grandchild?

"I gave my contact info to your housekeeper." The older
woman looked both shaken and determined. "Take good
care of Maggie. She's all I have left." And with more haste
than grace, Diane pulled her car door shut and started the
engine.

As the gray car backed down the driveway, Liam considered the decision his own mother had made, leaving
him and Kyle with her father to raise while she went off to
the life she wanted in Dallas. He'd never really felt a hole
in his life at her absence. Their grandfather had been an
ideal blend of tough and affectionate. No reason to think
that Maggie wouldn't do just as well without her mother.

He returned to the house. Candace was in the kitchen

warming a bottle of formula. The baby continued to show-case an impressive set of lungs. His housekeeper shot him a concerned glance.

"You let her go?" Candace rocked the baby.

"What was I supposed to do?"

"Convince her to take the baby with her?" She didn't sound all that certain. "You and I both know she isn't yours."

"You sound pretty sure about that."

Liam gave her a crooked smile. Candace had started working for him seven years ago when the former house-keeper retired. Diane Garner wasn't the first woman to show up unexpected and uninvited on his doorstep, al-though she was the first one to arrive with a baby.

"You've been different this last year." Candace eyed him. "More settled."

She'd never asked what had prompted his overnight transformation from carefree playboy to responsible busi-nessman. Maybe she figured with his thirtieth birthday he'd decided to leave his freewheeling days behind him. That was part of the truth, but not all.

"I've been living like a monk."

She grinned. "That, too."

"What am I supposed to do with a baby?" He eyed the red-faced infant with her wispy blond hair and unfocused blue eyes. "Why won't she stop crying?"

"She's not wet so I'm assuming she's hungry." Or maybe she just wants her mother. Candace didn't say the words, but the thought was written all over her face. "Can you hold her while I get her bottle ready?"

"I'd rather not."

"She won't break."

The child looked impossibly small in Candace's arms. Liam shook his head. "Tell me what to do to get a bottle ready."

The noise in the kitchen abated while the baby sucked greedily at her bottle. Liam made the most of this respite and contacted a local company that specialized in placing nannies. Since it wasn't quite seven in the morning, he was forced to leave a message and could only hope that he'd impressed the owners with the urgency of his need. That done, he set about creating a list of things that baby Maggie would need.

Hadley Stratton took her foot off the accelerator and let her SUV coast down the last thirty feet of driveway. An enormous Victorian mansion loomed before her, white siding and navy trim giving it the look of a graceful dowager in the rugged West Texas landscape.

The drive from her apartment in Royal had taken her fifteen minutes. Although a much shorter commute than her last job in Pine Valley, Hadley had reservations about taking the nanny position. Liam Wade had a playboy reputation, which made this the exact sort of situation she avoided. If he hadn't offered a salary at the top of her range and promised a sizable bonus if she started immediately, she would have refused when the agency called. But with student loans hanging over her head and the completion of her master's degree six short months away, Hadley knew she'd be a fool to turn down the money.

Besides, she'd learned her lesson when it came to attractive, eligible bosses. There would be no repeat of the mistake she'd made with Noah Heston, the divorced father of three who'd gone back to his ex-wife after enticing Hadley to fall in love with him.

Parking her SUV, Hadley headed for the front door and rang the bell. Inside a baby cried, and Hadley's agitation rose. She knew very little about the situation she was walking into. Only that Liam Wade had a sudden and urgent need for someone to care for an infant.

A shadow darkened the stained glass inset in the double door. When Hadley's pulse quickened, she suspected this was a mistake. For the last hour she'd been telling herself that Liam Wade was just like any other employer. Sure, the man was a world-class horseman and sexy as hell. Yes, she'd had a crush on him ten years ago, but so had most of the other teenage girls who barrel raced.

A decade had gone by. She was no longer a silly fangirl, but a mature, intelligent, *professional* nanny who knew the risks of getting emotionally wrapped up in her charges or their handsome fathers.

"Good morning, Mr. Wade." She spoke crisply as the door began to open. "Royal Nannies sent me. My name is—"

"Hadley…" His bottle-green eyes scanned her face.

"Hadley Stratton." Had he remembered her? No, of course not. "Stratton." She cleared her throat and tried not to sound as if her heart was racing. Of course he knew who she was; obviously the agency had let him know who they were sending. "I'm Hadley Stratton." She clamped her lips together and stopped repeating her name.

"You're a nanny?" He executed a quick but thorough assessment of her and frowned.

"Well, yes." Maybe he expected someone older. "I have my résumé and references if you'd like to look them over." She reached into her tote and pulled out a file.

"No need." He stepped back and gestured her inside. "Maggie's in the living room." He shut the door behind her and grimaced. "Just follow the noise."

Hadley didn't realize that she'd expected the baby's mother to be ridiculously young, beautiful and disinterested in motherhood until she spied the woman holding the child. In her late forties, she was wearing jeans, a flannel shirt and sneakers, her disheveled dark hair in a messy bun.

"Hadley Stratton. Candace Tolliver, my housekeeper."

Liam cast a fond grin at the older woman. "Who is very glad you've come so quickly."

Candace had the worn look of a first-time mother with a fussy baby. Even before the introductions were completed, she extended the baby toward Hadley. "I've fed her and changed her. She won't stop crying."

"What is her normal routine?" Hadley rocked and studied the tiny infant, wondering what had become of the child's mother. Smaller than the average newborn by a few pounds. Was that due to her mother's unhealthy nutritional habits while pregnant or something more serious?

"We don't know." Candace glanced toward Liam. "She only just arrived. Excuse me." She exited the room as if there were something burning in the kitchen.

"These are her medical records." Liam gestured toward a file on the coffee table. "Although she was premature, she checked out fine."

"How premature?" She slipped her pinkie between the infant's lips, hoping the little girl would try sucking and calm down. "Does she have a pacifier?"

Liam spoke up. "No."

Hadley glanced at him. He'd set one hand on his hip. The other was buried in his thick hair. He needed a haircut, she noted absently before sweeping her gaze around the room in search of the normal clutter that came with a child. Other than a car seat and a plastic bag from the local drugstore, the elegant but comfortable room looked like it belonged in a decorating magazine. Pale gray walls, woodwork painted a clean white. The furniture had accents of dusty blue, lime green and cranberry, relieving the monochrome palette.

"Where are her things?"

"Things?" The rugged horseman looked completely lost.

"Diapers, a blanket, clothes? Are they in her room?"

"She doesn't have a room."

"Then where does she sleep?"

"We have yet to figure that out."

Hadley marshaled her patience. Obviously there was a story here. "Perhaps you could tell me what's going on? Starting with where her mother is."

"She died a few days ago in a traffic accident."

"Oh, I'm sorry for your loss." Hadley's heart clenched as she gazed down at the infant who had grown calmer as she sucked on Hadley's finger. "The poor child never to know her mother."

Liam cleared his throat. "Actually, I didn't know her."

"You had to have…" Hadley trailed off. Chances were Liam Wade just didn't remember which one-night stand had produced his daughter. "What's your name, sweetheart?" she crooned, glad to see the infant's eyes closing.

"Maggie. Her mother was Margaret."

"Hello, little Maggie."

Humming a random tune, Hadley rocked Maggie. The combination of soothing noise and swaying motion put the baby to sleep, and Hadley placed her in the car seat.

"You are incredibly good at that."

Hadley looked up from tucking in the baby and found Liam Wade standing too close and peering over her shoulder at Maggie. The man smelled like pure temptation. If pure temptation smelled like soap and mouthwash. He wore jeans and a beige henley beneath his brown-and-cream plaid shirt. His boots were scuffed and well worn. He might be worth a pile of money, but he'd never acted as though it made him better than anyone else. He'd fit in at the horse shows he'd attended, ambling around with the rest of the guys, showing off his reining skills by snagging the flirts who stalked him and talking horses with men who'd been in the business longer than he'd been alive. His cockiness came from what he achieved on the back of a horse.

"This is the first time she's been quiet since she got here." His strained expression melted into a smile of devastating charm. "You've worked a miracle."

"Obviously not. She was just stressed. I suspect your tension communicated itself to her. How long has she been here?"

"Since about seven." Liam gestured her toward the black leather couch, but Hadley positioned herself in a black-and-white armchair not far from the sleeping child. "Her grandmother dropped her off and left."

"And you weren't expecting her?"

Liam shook his head and began to pace. "Perhaps I should start at the beginning."

"That might be best."

Before he could begin, his housekeeper arrived with a pot of coffee and two cups. After pouring for both, she glanced at the now-sleeping child, gave Hadley a thumbs-up and exited the room once more. Liam added sugar to his coffee and resumed his march around the room, mug in hand.

"Here's what I know. A woman arrived this morning with Maggie, said her name was Diane Garner and that her daughter had died after being in a car accident. Apparently she went into labor and lost control of the vehicle."

Hadley glanced at the sleeping baby and again sorrow overtook her. "That's just tragic. So where is her grandmother now?"

"On her way back to Houston, I'm sure."

"She left you with the baby?"

"I got the impression she couldn't handle the child or didn't want the responsibility."

"I imagine she thought the child was better off with her father."

"Maggie isn't mine." Liam's firm tone and resolute

expression encouraged no rebuttal. "She's my brother's child."

At first Hadley didn't know how to respond. Why would he have taken the child in if she wasn't his?

"I see. So I'll be working for your brother?" She knew little of the second Wade brother. Unlike Liam, he hadn't been active in reining or showing quarter horses.

"No, you'll be working for me. Kyle is in the military and lives on the East Coast."

"He's giving you guardianship of the child?"

Liam stared out the large picture window that over-looked the front lawn. "He's unreachable at the moment so I haven't been able to talk to him about what's going on. I'm not even sure Maggie is his."

This whole thing sounded too convoluted for Hadley's comfort. Was Liam Maggie's father and blaming his absent brother because he couldn't face the consequences of his actions? He wouldn't be the first man who struggled against facing up to his responsibilities. Her opinion of Liam Wade the professional horseman had always been high. But he was a charming scoundrel who was capable of seducing a woman without ever catching her name or collecting her phone number.

"I'm not sure I'm the right nanny for you," she began, her protest trailing off as Liam whirled from the window and advanced toward her.

"You are exactly what Maggie needs. Look at how peaceful she is. Candace spent two hours trying to calm her down, and you weren't here more than ten minutes and she fell asleep. Please stay. She lost her mother and obviously has taken to you."

"What you need is someone who can be with Maggie full-time. The clients I work with only need daytime help."

"The agency said you go to school."

"I'm finishing up my master's in child development."

"But you're off until the beginning of February when classes resume."

"Yes." She felt a trap closing in around her.

"That's four weeks away. I imagine we can get our situation sorted out by then, so we'd only need you during the day while I'm at the barn."

"And until then?"

"Would you be willing to move in here? We have more than enough room."

Hadley shook her head. She'd feel safer sleeping in her own bed. The thought popped into her mind unbidden. What made her think that she was in danger from Liam Wade? From what she knew of him, she was hardly his type.

"I won't move in, but I'll come early and stay late to give you as much time as you need during the month of January. In the meantime, you may want to consider hiring someone permanent."

Despite what Liam had said about Maggie being his brother's child, Hadley suspected the baby wasn't going anywhere once the DNA tests came back. With the child's mother dead and her grandmother unwilling to be responsible for her, Liam should just accept that he was going to need a full-time caregiver.

"That's fair."

Liam put out his hand, and Hadley automatically accepted the handshake. Tingles sped up her arm and raised the hair on the back of her neck as his firm grip lingered a few seconds longer than was professionally acceptable.

"Perhaps we could talk about the things that Maggie will need," Hadley said, hoping Liam didn't notice the odd squeak in her voice.

"Candace started a list. She said she'd get what we needed as soon as you arrived." His lips curved in a wry grin. "She didn't want to leave me alone with the baby."

"Why not?"

"It might seem strange to you, but I've never actually held a baby before."

Hadley tore her gaze away from the likable sparkle in Liam's arresting eyes. She absolutely could not find the man attractive. Hadley clasped her hands in her lap.

"Once you've held her for the first time, you'll see how easy it is." Seeing how deeply the baby was sleeping, Hadley decided this might be a great opportunity for him to begin. "And there's no time like the present."

Liam started to protest, but whatever he'd been about to say died beneath her steady gaze. "Very well." His jaw muscles bunched and released. "What do I do?"

Two

Going balls-out on a twelve-hundred-pound horse to chase down a fleeing cow required steady hands and a calm mind in the midst of a massive adrenaline rush. As a world-class trainer and exhibitor of reining and cutting horses, Liam prided himself on being the eye of the storm. But today, he was the rookie at his first rodeo and Hadley the seasoned competitor.

"It's important that you support her head." Hadley picked up the sleeping baby, demonstrating as she narrated. "Some babies don't like to be held on their backs, so if she gets fussy you could try holding her on her stomach or on her side."

Hadley came toward him and held out Maggie. He was assailed by the dual fragrances of the two females, baby powder and lavender. The scents filled his lungs and slowed his heartbeat. Feeling moderately calmer, Liam stood very still while Hadley settled Maggie into his arms.

"There." She peered at the sleeping child for a moment before lifting her eyes to meet Liam's gaze. Flecks of gold floated in her lapis-blue eyes, mesmerizing him with their sparkle. "See, that wasn't hard."

"You smell like lavender." The words passed his lips without conscious thought.

"Lavender and chamomile." She stepped back until her path was blocked by an end table. "It's a calming fragrance."

"It's working."

As he adjusted to the feel of Maggie's tiny body in his arms, he cast surreptitious glances Hadley's way. Did she remember him from her days of barrel racing? He hadn't seen her in ten years and often looked for her at the events he attended, half expecting her name to pop up among the winners. At eighteen she'd been poised to break out as a star in the barrel-racing circuit. And then she'd sold her mare and disappeared. Much to the delight of many of her competitors, chief among them Liam's on-again, off-again girlfriend.

"I almost didn't recognize you this morning," he said, shifting Maggie so he could free his right arm.

Hadley looked up at him warily. "You recognized me?"

How could she think otherwise? She'd been the one who'd gotten away. "Sure. You took my advice and won that sweepstakes class. You and I were supposed to have dinner afterward." He could tell she remembered that, even though she was shaking her head. "Only I never saw you again."

"I vaguely remember you trying to tell me what I was doing wrong."

"You had a nice mare. Lolita Slide. When you put her up for sale I told Shannon Tinger to buy her. She went on to make over a hundred thousand riding barrels with her."

"She was a terrific horse," Hadley said with a polite smile. "I'm glad Shannon did so well with her."

Liam remembered Hadley as a lanky girl in battered jeans and a worn cowboy hat, her blond hair streaming like a victory banner as her chestnut mare raced for the finish line. This tranquil woman before him, while lovely in gray dress pants and a black turtleneck sweater, pale hair pulled back in a neat ponytail, lacked the fire that had snagged his interest ten years earlier.

"We have a three-year-old son of Lolita's out in the barn.

You should come see him. I think he's going to make a first-class reining horse."

"I don't think there will be time. Infants require a lot of attention."

Her refusal surprised him. He'd expected her to jump at the chance to see what her former mount had produced. The Hadley he remembered had been crazy about horses.

"Why'd you quit?"

Hadley stared at the landscape painting over the fireplace while she answered Liam's blunt question. "My parents wanted me to go to college, and there wasn't money to do that and keep my horse. What I got for Lolita paid for my first year's tuition."

Liam considered her words. When was the last time he'd been faced with an either-or situation? Usually he got everything he wanted. Once in a while a deal didn't go his way, but more often than not, that left him open for something better.

Maggie began to stir, and Liam refocused his attention on the baby. Her lips parted in a broad yawn that accompanied a fluttering of her long lashes.

"I think she's waking up." He took a step toward Hadley, baby extended.

"You did very well for your first time."

Unsure if her tiny smile meant she was patronizing him, Liam decided he'd try harder to get comfortable with his niece. Strange as it was to admit it, he wanted Hadley's approval.

"Would you like a tour of the house?" Liam gestured toward the hallway. "I'd like your opinion on where to put the baby's room."

"Sure."

He led the way across the hall to the dining room. A long mahogany table, capable of seating twelve, sat on a black-and-gold Oriental rug. When he'd overhauled the house six years ago, bringing the plumbing and wiring up to code, this was the one room he'd left in its original state.

"It's just me living here these days, and I haven't entertained much in the last year." The reason remained a sore spot, but Liam brushed it aside. "When my grandfather was alive, he loved to host dinner parties. Several members of Congress as well as a couple governors have eaten here."

"When did you lose him?"

"A year and a half ago. He had a heart condition and died peacefully in his sleep." Grandfather had been the only parent he and Kyle had ever known, and his death had shaken Liam. How the loss had hit Kyle, Liam didn't know. Despite inheriting half the ranch when their grandfather died, his brother never came home and Liam dealt with him only once or twice a year on business matters.

"I remember your grandfather at the shows," Hadley said. "He always seemed larger than life."

Liam ushered her into the large modern kitchen. Her words lightened Liam's mood somewhat. "He loved the horse business. His father had been a cattleman. Our herd of Black Angus descends from the 1880s rush to bring Angus from Scotland."

"So you have both cattle and horses?"

"We have a Black Angus breeding program. Last year we sold two hundred two-year-olds."

"Sounds like you're doing very well."

After a quick peek in the den, they finished their tour of the first floor and climbed the stairs.

"Business has been growing steadily." So much so that Liam wasn't able to do what he really loved: train horses.

"You don't sound all that excited about your success."

He'd thought the abrupt cessation of his personal life would provide more time to focus on the ranch, but he'd discovered the more he was around, the more his staff came to him with ideas for expanding.

"I didn't realize how focused my grandfather had been on the horse side of the business until after his heart problems forced him into semiretirement. Apparently he'd been keeping things going out of respect for his father, but his heart wasn't really in it."

"And once he semiretired?"

"I hired someone who knew what he was doing and gave him a little capital. In three years he'd increased our profits by fifty percent." Liam led Hadley on a tour of three different bedrooms. "This one is mine."

"I think it would be best if Maggie is across the hall from you." Hadley had chosen a cheerful room with large windows overlooking the backyard and soft green paint on the walls. "That way when she wakes up at night you'll be close by."

While Liam wasn't worried about being up and down all night with the infant, he preferred not to be left alone in case something went wrong. "Are you sure I can't convince you to live in?"

"You'll do fine. I promise not to leave until I'm sure Maggie is well settled."

That was something, Liam thought. "If you have things under control for the moment, I need to get back to the barn. I have several calls to make and an owner stopping by to look at his crop of yearlings."

"Maggie and I will be fine."

"Candace should be back with supplies soon, and hopefully we'll have some baby furniture delivered later today. I'll have a couple of the grooms empty this room so it can be readied for Maggie."

Hadley nodded her approval. In her arms, the baby began to fuss. "I think it's time for a change and a little something to eat."

"Here's my cell and office numbers." Liam handed her his business card. "Let me know if you need anything."

"Thank you, I will."

The short drive back to the barn gave Liam a couple minutes to get his equilibrium back. Kyle was a father. That was going to shock the hell out of his brother.

And Liam had received a shock of his own today in the form of Hadley Stratton. Was it crazy that she was the one who stuck out in his mind when he contemplated past regrets? Granted, they'd been kids. He'd been twenty. She'd barely graduated high school the first time she'd made an impression on him. And it had been her riding that had caught his attention. On horseback she'd been a dynamo. Out of the saddle, she'd been quiet and gawky in a way he found very appealing.

He'd often regretted never getting the chance to know anything about her beyond her love of horses, and now fate had put her back in his life. Second chances didn't come often, and Liam intended to make the most of this one.

The grandfather clock in the entry hall chimed once as Hadley slipped through the front door into the cold night air. Shivering at the abrupt change in temperature, she trotted toward her SUV and slid behind the wheel. An enormous yawn cracked her jaw as she started the car and navigated the circular drive.

In order for Hadley to leave Liam in charge of Maggie, she'd had to fight her instincts. The baby was fussier than most, probably because she was premature, and only just went to sleep a little while ago. Although Liam had gained confidence as he'd taken his turn soothing the frazzled infant, Hadley had already grown too attached to the motherless baby and felt compelled to hover. But he needed to learn to cope by himself.

Weariness pulled at her as she turned the SUV on to the deserted highway and headed for Royal. Her last few assignments had involved school-age children, and she'd forgotten how exhausting a newborn could be. No doubt Liam would be weary beyond words by the time she returned at seven o'clock tomorrow morning.

This child, his daughter, was going to turn his world upside down. Already the house had a more lived-in feeling, less like a decorator's showplace and more like a family home. She wondered how it had been when Liam and his brother were young. No doubt the old Victorian had quaked with the noisy jubilance of two active boys.

Twenty minutes after leaving the Wade house, Hadley let herself into her one-bedroom apartment. Waldo sat on the front entry rug, appearing as if he'd been patiently awaiting her arrival for hours when in fact, the cat had probably been snoozing on her bed seconds earlier. As she shut the front door, the big gray tabby stretched grandly before trotting ahead of her toward the kitchen and his half-empty food bowl. Once it was filled to his satisfaction, Waldo sat down and began cleaning his face.

The drive had revived her somewhat. Hadley fixed herself a cup of Sleepytime tea and sipped at it as she checked the contents of the bags a good friend of hers had dropped off this afternoon. After seeing what Candace had bought for the baby, Hadley had contacted Kori to purchase additional supplies. She would owe her friend lunch once Maggie was settled in. Kori had shown horses when she was young and would get a kick out of hearing that Liam Wade was Hadley's new employer.

Hadley had a hard time falling asleep and barely felt as if she'd dozed for half an hour when her alarm went off at five. Usually she liked to work out in the morning and eat a healthy breakfast while watching morning news, but today she was anxious about how things had gone with Liam and Maggie.

Grabbing a granola bar and her to-go mug filled with coffee, Maggie retraced the drive she'd made a mere five hours earlier. The Victorian's second-floor windows blazed with light, and Hadley gave a huge sigh before shifting the SUV into Park and shutting off the engine.

The wail of a very unhappy baby greeted Hadley as she let herself in the front door. From the harried expression on Liam's face, the infant had been crying for some time.

"It doesn't sound as if things are going too well," she commented, striding into the room and holding out her arms for the baby. "Did you get any sleep?"

"A couple hours."

Liam was still dressed for bed in a pair of pajama bottoms that clung to his narrow hips and a snug T-shirt that highlighted a torso sculpted by physical labor. Hadley was glad to have the fussy baby to concentrate on. Liam's helplessness made him approachable, and that was dangerous. Even without his usual swagger, his raw masculinity was no less potent.

"Why don't you go back to bed and see if you can get a little more sleep?"

The instant she made the suggestion, Hadley wished the words back. She never told an employer what to do. Or she hadn't made that mistake since her first nanny job. She'd felt comfortable enough with Noah to step across the line that separated boss and friend. For a couple months that hadn't been a problem, but then she'd been pulled in too deep and had her heart broken.

"It's time I headed to the barn," Liam said, his voice muffled by the large hands he rubbed over his face. "There are a dozen things I didn't get to yesterday."

His cheeks and jaw were softened by a day's growth of beard, enhancing his sexy, just-got-out-of-bed look. Despite the distraction of a squirming, protesting child in her arms, Hadley registered a significant spike in her hormone levels. She wanted to run her palms over his broad shoulders and feel for herself the ripple of ab muscles that flexed as he scrubbed his fingers through his hair before settling his hands on his hips.

Light-headed, she sat down in the newly purchased rocking chair. Liam's effect on her didn't come as a surprise. She'd had plenty of giddy moments around him as a teenager. Once, after she'd had a particularly fantastic run, he'd even looked straight at her and smiled.

Hadley tightened her attention on Maggie and wrestled her foolishness into submission. Even if Liam was still that cocky boy every girl wanted to be with, she was no longer a susceptible innocent prone to bouts of hero worship. More important, he'd hired her to care for this baby, a child who was probably his daughter.

"Do you think she's okay?" Liam squatted down by the rocker. He gripped the arm of the chair to steady himself, his fingers brushing Hadley's elbow and sending ripples of sensation up her arm.

"You mean because she's been crying so much?" Hadley shot a glance at him and felt her resolve melting beneath the concern he showered on the baby. "I think she's just fussy. We haven't figured out exactly what she likes yet. It might take swaddling her tight or a certain sound that calms her. I used to take care of a baby boy who liked to fall asleep listening to the dishwasher."

"I know we talked about this yesterday," Liam began, his gaze capturing hers. "But can you make an exception for a few weeks and move in here?"

"I can't." The thought filled her with a mixture of excitement and panic. "I have a cat—"

"There's always plenty of mice in the barn."

Hadley's lips twitched as she imagined Waldo's horror at being cut off from the comforts of her bed and his favorite sunny spot where he watched the birds. "He's not that sort of cat."

"Oh." Liam gazed down at Maggie, who'd calmed

enough to accept a pacifier. "Then he can move in here with you."

Hadley sensed this was quite a compromise for Liam, but she still wasn't comfortable agreeing to stay in the house. "I think Maggie is going to be fine once she settles in a bit. She's been through a lot in the last few days."

"Look at her. She's been crying for three hours and you calm her down within five minutes. I can't go through another night like this one. You have to help me out. Ten days."

"A week." Hadley couldn't believe it when she heard herself bargaining.

Triumph blazed in Liam's eyes, igniting a broad smile. "Done." He got to his feet, showing more energy now that he'd gotten his way.

After a quick shower and a cup of coffee, Liam felt a little more coherent as he entered his bookkeeper/office manager's office. Ivy had been with Wade Ranch for nine years. She was a first cousin twice removed, and Grandfather had hired her as his assistant, and in a few short years her organizational skills had made her invaluable to the smooth running of the ranch.

"Tough night?" Ivy smirked at him over the rim of her coffee cup. She looked disgustingly chipper for seven in the morning. "Used to be a time when you could charm a female into doing your bidding."

Liam poured himself a cup of her wickedly strong brew and slumped onto her couch. "I'm rusty." Although he'd persuaded Hadley to move in for a week. Maybe it was just babies that were immune.

"Have you considered what you're going to do if the baby isn't Kyle's?"

As Ivy voiced what had filtered through Liam's mind several times during the last twenty-four hours, he knew he'd better contact a lawyer today. Technically, unless he claimed the child as his, he had no legal rights to her.

"I really believe Kyle is her father," Liam said. "I'm heading to a clinic Hadley recommended to have a DNA test run. I figured since Kyle and I are identical twins, the results should come back looking like Maggie is my daughter."

And then what? Margaret was dead. With Kyle estranged from his family, it wasn't likely he or Maggie would spend much time at Wade Ranch. And if Liam was wrong about his brother being Maggie's father, Diane Garner might give her up to strangers.

Liam was surprised how fast he'd grown attached to the precious infant; the idea of not being in her life bothered him. But was he ready to take on the challenge of fatherhood? Sure, he and Kyle had done okay raised by their grandfather, but could a little girl be raised by a man alone? Wouldn't she miss a mother snuggling her, brushing her hair and teaching her all the intricacies of being a woman? And yet it wasn't as if Liam would stay single forever.

An image of Hadley flashed through his thoughts. Beautiful, nurturing and just stubborn enough to be interesting. A year ago he might not have given her a second thought. Hadley was built for steady, long-term relationships, not the sort of fun and games that defined Liam's private life. She'd probably be good for him, but would he be good for her? After a year of celibacy, his libido was like an overwound spring, ready to explode at the least provocation.

"Liam, are you listening to me?" Ivy's sharp tone shattered his thoughts.

"No. Sorry. I was thinking about Maggie and the future."

Her expression shifted to understanding. "Why don't we

talk later this afternoon. You have a fund-raising meeting at the club today, don't you?"

He'd forgotten all about it. Liam had been involved with the Texas Cattleman's Club fund-raising efforts for Royal Memorial's west wing ever since it had been damaged by a tornado more than a year ago. The grand reopening was three weeks away, but there remained several unfinished projects to discuss.

"I'll be back around three."

"See you then."

Fearing if he sat down in his large office, he might doze off, Liam headed into the attached barn where twelve champion American quarter horse stallions stood at stud. Three of them belonged to Wade Ranch; the other nine belonged to clients.

Liam was proud of all they'd accomplished and wished that his grandfather had lived to see their annual auction reach a record million dollars for 145 horses. Each fall they joined with three other ranches to offer aged geldings, sought after for their proven ranch performance, as well as some promising young colts and fillies with top bloodlines.

At the far end of the barn, double doors opened into a medium-sized indoor arena used primarily for showing clients' horses. One wall held twenty feet of glass windows. On the other side was a spacious, comfortable lounge used for entertaining the frequent visitors to the ranch. A large television played videos of his stallions in action as well as highlights from the current show and racing seasons.

Liam went through the arena and entered the show barn. Here is where he spent the majority of his time away from ranch business. He'd grown up riding and training reining horses and had won dozens of national titles as well as over a million dollars in prize money before he'd turned twenty-five.

Not realizing his destination until he stood in front of

the colt's stall, Liam slid open the door and regarded WR Electric Slide, son of Hadley's former mount, Lolita. The three-year-old chestnut shifted in the stall and pushed his nose against Liam's chest. Chuckling, he scratched the colt's cheek, and his mind returned to Hadley.

While he understood that college and grad school hadn't left her the time or the money to own a horse any longer, it didn't make sense the way she'd shot down his suggestion that she visit this son of her former mount. And he didn't believe that she'd lost interest in horses. Something more was going on, and he wasn't going to let it go.

Three

Hadley sat in the nursery's comfortable rocking chair with Maggie on her lap, lightly tapping her back to encourage the release of whatever air she'd swallowed while feeding. It was 3:00 a.m., and Hadley fended off the house's heavy silence by quietly humming. The noise soothed the baby and gave Hadley's happiness a voice.

She'd been living in the Wade house for three days, and each morning dawned a little brighter than the last. The baby fussed less. Liam smiled more. And Hadley got to enjoy Candace's terrific cooking as well as a sense of accomplishment.

Often the agency sent her to handle the most difficult situations, knowing that she had a knack for creating cooperation in the most tumultuous of households. She attributed her success to patience, techniques she'd learned in her child development classes and determination. Preaching boundaries and cooperation, she'd teach new habits to the children and demonstrate to the parents how consistency made their lives easier.

Feeling more than hearing Maggie burp, Hadley resettled the baby on her back and picked up the bottle once more. Her appetite had increased after her pediatrician diagnosed acid reflux, probably due to her immature digestive system, and prescribed medication to neutralize her stomach acids. Now a week old, Maggie had stopped losing weight and was almost back to where she'd started.

In addition to the reflux problem, Maggie had symptoms of jaundice. Dr. Stringer had taken blood samples to run for DNA, and the bilirubinometer that tested jaundice levels had shown a higher-than-average reading. To Liam's dismay, the doctor had suggested they wait a couple weeks to see if the jaundice went away on its own. He'd only relaxed after the pediatrician suggested they'd look at conventional phototherapy when the blood tests came back.

By the time Hadley settled Maggie back into her crib, it was almost four in the morning. With the late-night feedings taking longer than average because of Maggie's reflux problem, Hadley had gotten in the habit of napping during the day when the baby slept. The abbreviated sleep patterns were beginning to wear on her, but in four short days she would be back spending the night in her tiny apartment once more.

Yawning into her pajama sleeve, Hadley shuffled down the hall to her room. Seeing that her door was open brought her back to wakefulness. In her haste to reach Maggie before she awakened Liam, Hadley hadn't pulled her door fully shut, and after a quick check under the bed and behind the chair, she conceded that the cat was missing. Damn. She didn't want to tiptoe around the quiet house in search of a feline who enjoyed playing hide-and-seek. Given the size of the place, she could be at it for hours.

Silently cursing, Hadley picked up a pouch of kitty treats and slipped out of her room. The floorboards squeaked beneath her. Moving with as much stealth as possible, she stole past Liam's room and headed toward the stairs.

Once on the first floor, Hadley began shaking the treat bag and calling Waldo's name in a stage whisper. She began in the living room, peering under furniture and trying not to sound as frustrated as she felt. No cat. Next, she moved on to the den. That, too, was feline free. After a quick and fruitless sweep of the dining room, she headed into the kitchen, praying Waldo had found himself a perch on top of the refrigerator or made a nest in the basket of dirty clothes in the laundry room. She found no sign of the gray tabby anywhere.

Hadley returned to the second floor, resigned to let the cat find his own way back, hoping he did before Liam woke up. But as she retraced her steps down the dim corridor, she noticed something that had eluded her earlier. Liam's door was open just wide enough for a cat to slip inside. She paused in the hall and stared at the gap. Had it been like that when she'd passed by earlier? It would be just like Waldo to gravitate toward the one person in the house who didn't like him.

She gave the pouch of cat treats a little shake. The sound was barely above a whisper, but Waldo had fantastic hearing, and while he might disregard her calls, he never ignored his stomach. Hadley held her breath for a few tense, silent seconds and listened for the patter of cat paws on the wood floor, but heard nothing but Liam's deep, rhythmic breathing. Confident that he was sound asleep, she eased open his door until she could slip inside.

Her first step into Liam's bedroom sent alarm bells shrilling in her head. Had she lost her mind? She was sneaking into her employer's room in the middle of the night while he slept. How would she explain herself if he woke? Would he believe that she was in search of her missing cat or would he assume she was just another opportunistic female? As the absurdity of the situation hit her, Hadley pressed her face into the crook of her arm and smothered a giggle. Several deep breaths later she had herself mostly back under control and advanced another careful step into Liam's room.

Her eyes had long ago grown accustomed to the darkness, and the light of a three-quarter moon spilled through the large window, so it was easy for her to make out the modern-looking king-size bed and the large man sprawled beneath the pale comforter. And there was Waldo, lying on top of Liam's stomach looking for all the world as if he'd found the most comfortable place on earth. He stared at Hadley, the tip of his tail sweeping across Liam's chin in a subtle taunt.

This could not be happening.

Hadley shook the pouch gently and Waldo's gold eyes narrowed, but he showed no intention of moving. Afraid that Liam would wake if she called the cat, Hadley risked approaching the bed. He simply had to move on his own. In order to pick him up, she'd have to slide her hand between Waldo's belly and Liam's stomach. Surely that would wake the sleeping man.

Pulling out a treat, she waved it in front of the cat's nose. Waldo's nose twitched with interest, but he displayed typical catlike disdain for doing anything expected of him. He merely blinked and glanced away. Could she snatch up the cat and make it to the door before Liam knew what had happened? Her mind ran through the possibilities and saw nothing but disaster.

Maybe she could nudge the cat off Liam. She poked the cat's shoulder. Waldo might have been glued where he lay. Working carefully, she slid her finger into his armpit and prodded upward, hoping to annoy him into a sitting position. He resisted by turning his body to stone.

Crossing her fingers that Liam was as sound a sleeper as he appeared, Hadley tried one last gambit. She scratched Waldo's head and was rewarded by a soft purr. Now that he was relaxed, she slid her nails down his spine and was rewarded when he pushed to his feet, the better to enjoy the caress. Leaning farther over the mattress, she slid one hand behind his front legs and cupped his butt in her other palm when she felt the air stir the fabric of her pajama top against her skin.

Hadley almost yelped as a large hand skimmed beneath the hem of her top and traced upward over her rib cage to the lower curve of her breast. Awkwardly looming over Liam's bed, her hands wrapped around an increasingly unhappy feline, she glanced at Liam's face and noticed that while his eyes remained closed, one corner of his lips had lifted into a half smile.

Liam was having an amazing dream. He lay on a couch in front of a roaring fire with a woman draped across him. Her long hair tickled his chin as his hands swept under her shirt, fingers tracing her ribs. Her bare skin was warm and soft beneath his caress and smelled like lavender and vanilla.

It was then he realized whom he held. He whispered her name as his palm discovered the swell of her breast. His fingertips grazed across her tight nipple and her body quivered in reaction, He smiled. A temptress lurked beneath her professional reserve and he was eager to draw her out. Before he could caress further, however, something landed on his chest with a thump.

The dream didn't so much dissolve as shatter. One second he was inches away from heaven, the next he was sputtering after having his breath knocked out. His eyes shot open. Darkness greeted him. His senses adjusted as wakefulness returned.

The silken skin from his dream was oh so real against his fingers. As was the disturbed breathing that disrupted the room's silence.

"Hadley?"

She was looming over his bed, frozen in place, her arms extended several inches above his body. "Waldo got out of my room and came in here. I was trying to lift him off you when you…" Her voice trailed off. She gathered the large gray cat against her chest and buried her face in his fur.

Liam realized his hand was still up her pajama top, palm resting against her side, thumb just below the swell of her breast. The willpower it took to disengage from the compromising position surprised him.

"I was dreaming…" He sat up in bed and rubbed his face to clear the lingering fog of sleep. "Somehow you got tangled up in it."

"You were dreaming of me?" She sounded more dismayed than annoyed.

He reached for the fading dream and confirmed that she had been the object of his passion. "No." She'd already pegged him as a womanizer; no need to add fuel to the fire. "The woman in my dream wasn't anyone I knew."

"Perhaps it was Margaret Garner."

It frustrated him that she continued to believe Maggie was his daughter. "That's possible, since I never met her." His tone must have reflected his frustration because Hadley stepped away from his bed.

"I should get back to my room. Sorry we woke you."

"No problem." Liam waited until the door closed behind her before he toppled backward onto the mattress.

The sheer insanity of the past few moments made him grin. Had she really sneaked into his room to fetch the cat? Picturing what must have happened while he slept made him chuckle. He wished he could have seen her face. He'd bet she'd blushed from her hairline to her toes. Hadley didn't have the brazen sensuality of the women who usually caught his interest. She'd never show up half dressed in his hotel room and pout because he'd rather watch a football game than fool around. Nor would she stir up gossip in an attempt to capture his attention. She was such a straight arrow. Her honesty both captivated and alarmed him.

Rather than stare sleepless at the ceiling, Liam laid his

forearm over his eyes and tried to put Hadley out of his mind. However, vivid emotions had been stirred while he'd been unconscious. Plus, he was having a hard time forgetting the oh-so-memorable feel of her soft skin. With his body in such a heightened state of awareness, there was no way Liam was going to just fall back asleep. Cursing, he rolled out of bed and headed for the shower. Might as well head to the barn and catch up on paperwork.

Three hours later he'd completed the most pressing items and headed out to the barn to watch the trainers work the two-year-olds. At any time, there were between twenty and thirty horses in various stages of training.

They held classes and hosted clinics. For the last few years, Liam had taught a group of kids under ten years old who wanted to learn the ins and outs of competitive reining. They were a steely-eyed bunch of enthusiasts who were more serious about the sport than many adults. At the end of every class, he thanked heaven it would be a decade before he had to compete against them.

"Hey, boss. How're the colts looking?" Jacob Stevens, Liam's head trainer, had joined him near the railing.

"Promising." Liam had been watching for about an hour. "That bay colt by Blue is looking better all the time."

"His full brother earned over a quarter of a million. No reason to think Cielo can't do just as well." Jacob shot his boss a wry grin. "Think you're going to hold on to him?"

Liam laughed. "I don't know. I've been trying to limit myself to keeping only five in my name. At the moment, I own eight."

Until Hadley had shown up, he'd been seriously contemplating selling Electric Slide. The colt was going to be a champion, but Liam had more horses than he had time for. If only he could convince Hadley to get back in the saddle. He knew she'd balk at being given the horse, but maybe she'd be willing to work him as much as time permitted.

"Thing is," Jacob began, "you've got a good eye, and the ranch keeps producing winners."

Liam nodded. "It's definitely a quality problem. I've had a couple of good offers recently. Maybe I need to stop turning people down."

"Or just wait for the right owner."

"Speaking of that. Can you get one of the guys to put Electric Slide through his paces? I want to get some video for a friend of mine."

"Sure."

As he recorded the chestnut colt, Liam wasn't sure if he'd have any luck persuading Hadley to come check out the horse, but he really wanted to get to the bottom of her resistance.

Lunchtime rolled around, and Liam headed back to the house. He hadn't realized how eager he was to spend some time with Maggie and Hadley until he stopped his truck on the empty driveway and realized Hadley's SUV was absent.

Candace was pulling a pie out of the oven as he entered the kitchen. Her broad smile faded as she read the expression on his face. "What's wrong?"

"Where's Hadley?"

"Shopping for clothes and things for Maggie." Candace set a roast beef sandwich on the center island and went to the refrigerator for a soda. "The poor girl hasn't been out of here in days."

"She took Maggie with her?"

"I offered to watch her while she was gone, but the weather is warm, and Hadley thought the outing would do her some good."

"How long have they been gone?"

"About fifteen minutes." Candace set her hands on her hips and regarded him squarely. "Is there some reason for all the questions?"

"No."

Liam wondered at his edginess. He trusted Maggie was in good hands with Hadley, but for some reason, the thought of both of them leaving the ranch had sparked his anxiety. What was wrong with him? It wasn't as if they weren't ever coming back.

The thought caught him by surprise. Is that what was in the back of his mind? The notion that people he cared about left the ranch and didn't come back? Ridiculous. Sure, his mother had left him and Kyle. And then Kyle had gone off to join the navy, but people needed to live their lives. It had nothing to do with him or the ranch. Still, the sense of uneasiness lingered.

Royal Diner was humming with lunchtime activity when Hadley pushed through the glass door in search of a tuna melt and a chance to catch up with Kori. To her relief, her best friend had already snagged one of the booths. Hadley crossed the black-and-white checkerboard floor and slid onto the red faux-leather seat with a grateful sigh.

"I'm so glad you were able to meet me last-minute," Hadley said, settling Maggie's carrier beside her and checking on the sleeping infant.

She'd already fed and changed the baby at Priceless, Raina Patterson's antiques store and craft studio. Hadley had taken a candle-making class there last month and wanted to see what else Raina might be offering.

"Thanks for calling. This time of year is both a blessing and a curse." Kori was a CPA who did a lot of tax work, making January one of her slower months. "I love Scott, but his obsessive need to be busy at all times gets on my nerves." Kori and her husband had started their accounting company two years ago, and despite what she'd just said, the decision had been perfect for them.

"You're the one doing me a favor. I really need your

advice." Hadley trailed off as the waitress brought two Diet Cokes.

They put in their lunch order and when the waitress departed, Kori leaned her forearms on the table and fixed Hadley with an eager stare.

"This is fantastic. You never need my help with anything."

Her friend's statement caught Hadley off guard. "That's not true. I'm always asking for favors."

"Little things, sure, like when you asked me to pick up baby stuff for Miss Maggie or help with your taxes, but when it comes to life stuff you're so self-sufficient." Kori paused. "And I'm always boring you with the stuff that I'm going through."

Hadley considered. "I guess I've been focused on finishing my degree and haven't thought much beyond that. Plus, it's not like I have a social life to speak of."

Kori waved her hands. "Forget all that. Tell me what's going on."

Embarrassment over her early-morning encounter with Liam hadn't faded one bit. Her skin continued to tingle in the aftermath of his touch while other parts of her pulsed with insistent urgency. The only thing that kept her from quitting on the spot was that he'd been asleep when he'd slid his hand beneath her clothes.

"Oh my goodness," Kori exclaimed in awe. "You're blushing."

Hadley clapped her hands over her cheeks. "Am I?"

"What happened?"

"Waldo got out of my room last night when I got up for Maggie's feeding, and when I tracked him down, he was in Liam's room, curled up right here." Hadley indicated where her cat had been on Liam's anatomy.

"You said he isn't a cat person. Was he mad?"

"He was asleep."

Kori began to laugh. "So what happened?"

"I tried to lure him off with a treat, but Waldo being Waldo wouldn't budge. As I was picking him up…" Swept by mortification, Hadley closed her eyes for a span of two heartbeats.

"Yes?" Kori's voice vibrated with anticipation. "You picked him up and what?"

"I was leaning over the bed and Liam was sleeping. And dreaming." Hadley shuddered. "About having sex with some woman, I think."

"And?" Kori's delighted tone prompted Hadley to spill the next part of her tale.

"The next thing I knew, his hand was up my shirt and he—" she mimed a gesture "—my breast." Her voice trailed off in dismay.

"No way. And you're sure he was asleep?"

"Positive. Unfortunately, I was so shocked that I didn't keep a good hold of Waldo and he jumped onto Liam's chest, waking him. I don't think he knew what hit him."

"What did he say?"

"I honestly don't remember. I think I mumbled an apology for waking him. He retrieved his hand from beneath my pajama top and I bolted with Waldo."

"Did you talk to him later?"

"He was gone before Maggie woke up again, and then I took off before he came home for lunch." Hadley glanced at her charge to make sure the baby was sleeping soundly. "What am I supposed to say or do the next time I see him?"

"You could thank him for giving you the best sex you've had in years."

"We didn't have sex." Hadley lowered her voice and hissed the last word, scowling at her friend.

"It's the closest thing you've had to a physical encounter in way too long." Kori fluffed her red hair and gazed in disgust at her friend. "I don't know how you've gone so long without going crazy. If Scott and I go three days without sex we become vile, miserable people."

Hadley rolled her eyes at her friend. "I'm not in a committed, monogamous relationship. You and Scott have been together for seven years. You've forgotten how challenging being single is. And if you recall, the last time I fell in love it didn't work out so well."

"Noah was an ass. He led you on while he was still working through things with his ex-wife."

"She wanted him back," Hadley reminded her friend. "He'd never stopped loving her even after finding out she'd cheated on him. And he was thinking about his kids."

"He still hedged his bets with you. At the very least, he should have told you where things stood between them."

On that, Hadley agreed. Five years earlier, she'd been a blind fool to fall in love with Noah. Not only had he been her employer, but also things had moved too fast between them. Almost immediately he'd made her feel like a part of the family. Because it was her first time being a nanny, she hadn't understood that his behavior had crossed a line. She'd merely felt accepted and loved.

"That was a long time ago." Thinking about Noah made her sad and angry. He'd damaged her ability to trust and opened a hole in her heart that had never healed. "Can we get back to my more immediate problem? Do I quit?"

"Because your boss sleep–felt you up?" Kori shook her head. "Chalk it up to an embarrassing mistake and forget about it."

"You're right." Only she was having a hard time forgetting how much she enjoyed his hands on her skin. In fact, she wanted him to run his hands all over her body and make her come for him over and over.

Kori broke into her thoughts. "You're thinking about him right now, aren't you?"

"What?" Hadley sipped at her cold drink, feeling overly warm. "No. Why would you think that?"

"You've got the hots for him. Good for you."

"No. Not good for me. He's my boss, for one thing. For another, he's a major player. I knew him when I used to race barrels. He had girls chasing after him all the time, and he enjoyed every second of it."

"So he's a playboy. You don't need to fall in love with him, just scratch an itch."

"I can't." Hadley gave her head a vehement shake to dispel the temptation of Kori's matter-of-fact advice. "Besides, I'm not his type. He was asleep during most of what happened this morning."

"Wait. Most?"

Hadley waved to dismiss her friend's query. "It might have taken him a couple extra seconds to move his hand."

Kori began to laugh again. "Oh, he must have really been thrown for a loop. You in his bedroom in the middle of the night with the cat."

The picture Kori painted was funny, and Hadley let herself laugh. "Thank you for putting the whole thing in perspective. I don't know why I was so stressed about it."

"Maybe because despite your best intentions, you like the guy more than you think you should."

Hadley didn't even bother to deny it. "Maybe I do," she said. "But it doesn't matter, because no matter how attractive I may find him, he's my boss, and you know I'm never going there again."

Four

After missing Maggie and Hadley at lunchtime, Liam made sure he was home, showered and changed early enough to spend some time with his niece before dinner. She was in her crib and just beginning to wake up when he entered her room. Hadley wasn't there, but he noticed the red light on the baby monitor and suspected she was in her room or downstairs, keeping one ear tuned to the receiver.

Before Maggie could start to fuss, Liam scooped her out of the crib and settled her on the changing table. Already he was becoming an expert with the snaps and Velcro fastenings of Maggie's Onesies and diapers. Before the baby came fully awake, he had her changed and nestled in his arm on the way downstairs.

The domestic life suited him, he decided, entering the kitchen to see what Candace had made for dinner. The large room smelled amazing, and his mouth began to water as soon as he crossed the threshold. He sneaked up behind Candace and gave her a quick hug.

"What's on the menu tonight?"

"I made a roast. There's garlic mashed potatoes, green beans and apple pie for dessert."

"And your wonderful gravy."

"Of course."

"Is Jacob joining us?"

"Actually, we're going to have dinner in town. It's the seventh anniversary of our first date."

Candace and Jacob had been married for the last six years. They'd met when Candace had come to work at Wade Ranch and fell in love almost at first sight. They had the sort of solid relationship that Liam had never had the chance to see as he was growing up.

"You keep track of that sort of thing?" Liam teased, watching as Candace began fixing Maggie's bottle.

"It's keeping track of that sort of thing that keeps our relationship healthy."

Liam accepted the bottle Candace handed him, his thoughts wrapped around what she'd said. "What else keeps your relationship healthy?"

If the seriousness of his tone surprised her, the housekeeper didn't let on. "Trust and honesty. Jacob and I agreed not to let things fester. It's not always easy to talk about what bugs us, especially big issues like his sister's negative attitude toward me and the fact that I hate holding hands in public. Thank goodness we're both morning people and like the same television shows, or we'd never have made it this far."

As Liam watched Maggie suck down the formula, he let Candace's words wash over him. He'd never actually been in a relationship, healthy or otherwise. Oh, he dated a lot of women, some of them for long periods of time, but as he'd realized a year ago, not one of them wanted more than to have a good time.

At first he'd been shocked to discover that he'd let his personal life remain so shallow. Surely a thirty-year-old man should have had at least one serious relationship he could look back on. Liam hadn't been able to point to a single woman who'd impacted his life in any way.

He didn't even have mommy issues, because he'd never gotten to know her. She was a distracted, preoccupied guest at Christmas or when she showed up for his birthday. When she couldn't make it, expensive presents arrived and were dutifully opened. The most up-to-date electronics, gift cards, eventually big checks. For Liam, their mother had been the beautiful young woman in the photo framed by silver that sat on Grandfather's desk. According to him, she'd loved her career more than anything else and wasn't cut out to live on a ranch.

"...and of course, great sex."

The last word caught his attention. Liam grinned. "Of course."

Candace laughed. "I wondered if you were listening to me. Turns out you weren't."

"I was thinking about my past relationships or lack thereof."

"You just haven't found the right girl." Candace patted him on the arm, adopting the persona of wise old aunt. "Once she shows up, you'll have all the relationship you can handle. Just remember to think about her happiness before your own and you'll be all right."

Liam thought about his past girlfriends and knew that advice would have bankrupted him. His former lovers wanted the best things money could buy. Expensive clothes, exotic trips, to be pampered and spoiled. Living such an affluent lifestyle had been fine for short periods of time, but at heart, Liam loved the ranch and his horses. None of his lady friends wanted to live in Royal permanently. It was too far from the rapid pace of city life.

"I'm out of here," Candace said, slipping her coat off the hook near the kitchen door. "You and Hadley should be able to handle things from here. See you tomorrow." She winked. "Probably for lunch. You'll have your choice of cereal or Pop-Tarts for breakfast."

Grimacing, Liam wished her a good night and returned his attention to Maggie. The greedy child had consumed almost the entire bottle while he'd been talking to Candace. Knowing he should have burped her halfway through, he slung a towel over his shoulder and settled her atop it. Hadley's simple ways of handling Maggie's reflux issues had made a huge difference in the baby's manner. She was much less fussy.

Liam walked around the kitchen, swaying with each stride to soothe the infant. He'd been at this for ten minutes when Hadley entered the room. She'd left her hair down tonight, and the pale gold waves cascaded over the shoulders of her earth-tone blanket coat. The weather had turned chilly and wet in the early evening, and Hadley had dressed accordingly in jeans and a dark brown turtleneck sweater.

"Have you already fed her?" Hadley approached and held her hands out for the baby. She avoided meeting his gaze as she said, "I can take her while you eat."

"Maggie and I are doing fine." The baby gave a little burp as if in agreement. "Why don't you fix yourself a plate while I give her the rest of her bottle? I can eat after you're done."

Hadley looked as if she wanted to argue with him, but at last gave a little nod. "Sure."

While he pretended to be absorbed in feeding Maggie, Liam watched Hadley, thinking about their early-morning encounter and wondering if that accounted for her skittishness. Had he done more while asleep than she'd let on? The thought brought with it a rush of heat. He bit back a smile. Obviously his subconscious had been working overtime.

"Look, about this morning—" he began, compelled to clear the air.

"You were sleeping." Hadley's shoulders drooped. "I intruded. I swear I won't let Waldo get out again."

"Maybe it's not good for him to be cooped up all the time."

"My apartment is pretty small. Besides, you don't like cats."

"What makes you say that?" Liam had no real opinion either way.

Hadley crossed her arms over her chest and gave him the sort of stern look he imagined she'd give a disobedient child. "You suggested I put him in the barn."

"My grandfather never wanted animals in the house, so that's what I'm used to."

"The only time Waldo has been outside was after the house where he lived was destroyed by the tornado. He spent a month on his own before someone brought him to Royal Haven, where I adopted him. He gets upset if I leave him alone too long. That's why I couldn't stay here without bringing him."

Talking about her cat had relaxed Hadley. She'd let down her guard as professional caretaker, and Liam found himself charmed by her fond smile and soft eyes. No wonder she had such a magical effect on Maggie. She manifested a serenity that made him long to nestle her body against his and...

Desire flowed through him, brought on by a year of celibacy and Hadley's beauty. But was that all there was to it? Over the last year, he hadn't been a hermit. Promoting the ranch meant he'd attended several horse shows, toured numerous farms. Every public appearance provided opportunities to test his resolve, but not one of the women he'd met had tempted him like Hadley.

Liam cleared his throat, but the tightness remained. "Why don't you bring him down after dinner so he and I can meet properly and then let him have the run of the house?"

"Are you sure?"

He'd made the suggestion impulsively, distracted by

the direction his thoughts had taken, but it was too late to change his mind now. "Absolutely."

The exchange seemed to banish the last of her uneasiness. Unfortunately, his discomfort had only just begun. Maggie had gone still in his arms, and Liam realized she was on the verge of sleep. Knowing her reflux required her to remain upright for half an hour, he shifted her onto his shoulder and followed Hadley to the kitchen table where he ate most of his meals since his grandfather had died.

"Is something the matter?" Hadley asked. She'd carried both their plates to the table.

"No, why?"

"You're frowning." She sat down across from him. "Do you want me to take Maggie?"

"No, she's fine." In less than a week he'd mastered the ability to hold the baby and do other things at the same time. He picked up his fork. "I was just thinking that I haven't used the dining room much since my grandfather died. Every meal he ate in this house was in there. I find it too big and lonely to use by myself."

"You could eat there with Maggie."

"*We* could eat there with Maggie."

Her eyes widened briefly before she gave a reluctant nod. "Of course, I would be there to take care of Maggie."

Liam didn't think they were on the same page. He'd been thinking of her in terms of companionship. She'd obviously assumed he'd want her as Maggie's caretaker. Or was she deliberately reminding him of their different roles in the household?

"I promised I'd bring Maggie down to the barn tomorrow for a visit. I'd like you to come with us." Now that the DNA results had come back indicating that Maggie was Kyle's daughter, he was eager to introduce her to everyone.

"Of course." Hadley didn't sound overly enthusiastic.

"She's a Wade, which means she's going to be spending a lot of time there."

"Or she may take after…my mother. She left the ranch to pursue a career in real estate and rarely visits." He had no idea what had prompted him to share this about his mother.

"Not everyone is cut out for this life, I suppose."

Or for motherhood. She'd left her sons in the care of their grandfather and hadn't returned more than a handful of times during their childhood. Liam knew it had bothered Grandfather that his only child didn't want anything to do with her family's legacy. As for how Kyle felt, Liam and his brother rarely discussed her.

"You mentioned that you're finishing up your degree. What are your plans for after graduation?"

Hadley smiled. "I've submitted my résumé to several school districts in Houston. That's where my parents live."

"You're not planning on staying in Royal then?"

"I like it here. My best friend and her husband run an accounting firm in town. I'm just not sure there are enough job opportunities in the area for someone just starting out in my field. And I'm an only child. My parents hate that I live so far away."

"What sort of a job are you looking for?" Liam found himself wanting to talk her into remaining in the area.

"School counseling. My undergraduate degree is in teaching, but after a couple years, I decided it wasn't my cup of tea and went back for my master's."

"You're certainly good with children," Liam said. "Any school would be lucky to have you."

While they spoke, Hadley had finished eating. She took charge of Maggie, settling her into the nearby infant seat while Liam finished his dinner. He made short work of Candace's excellent cooking and set both of their plates in the sink.

"Can I interest you in a piece of caramel apple pie? Candace makes the best around."

"Sure." Hadley laughed. "I have a weakness for dessert."

Liam heated both pieces in the microwave and added a scoop of ice cream to each. With Maggie sound asleep, she no longer provided any sort of distraction, and Liam was able to focus his full attention on Hadley.

"I took some video of Electric Slide being worked today. Thought you might be interested in seeing him in action." He pulled up the footage he'd taken with his phone and extended it her way. "Even though he's young, I can already tell he has his mother's work ethic and athleticism. I'd love your opinion on him."

"You're the expert," she reminded him, cupping the phone in her hands.

"Yes, but as I was discussing with my head trainer today, I have too many horses, and I need to figure out which ones I should let go."

"You're thinking of selling him?" She looked up from the phone's screen, her expression concerned.

And with that, Liam knew he'd struck the right chord at last.

Knowing she shouldn't care one way or another what Liam did with his horses, Hadley let her gaze be drawn back to the video of the big chestnut colt racing across the arena only to drop his hindquarters and execute a somewhat sloppy sliding stop. His inexperience showed, but she liked his balance and his willingness.

Lolita had been a dream horse. For two years she and Hadley had dominated as barrel racers and scored several championships in the show ring. During that time she'd had several offers to purchase the mare but couldn't imagine being parted from her.

Until Anna's accident, when everything changed.

"He's a nice colt," she said, making an effort to keep her reply noncommittal. She replayed the video, paying close attention to the horse's action. He looked so much like his mother. Same three white socks. Same shoulder and hip. Same nose-out gesture when he moved from a lope into a gallop. How many classes had she lost before that little quirk had been addressed?

"Maybe you can give him a try when you come to the barn tomorrow."

Her stomach tightened as she contemplated how much fun it would be to ride Lolita's son. But Hadley hadn't been on a horse in ten years, not since Anna had ended up in a wheelchair. Remorse over her role in what happened to her friend had burdened Hadley for a decade. The only thing that kept her from being overwhelmed by guilt was her vow never to ride again. And that was a small sacrifice compared with what Anna was living with.

"I'm afraid I don't ride anymore."

"I'm sure you haven't lost any of your skills."

Hadley found dark amusement in his confidence. She was pretty sure any attempt to swing into a saddle would demonstrate just how rusty she was.

"The truth is I don't want to ride." She didn't think Liam would understand her real reason for turning him down.

"But you might enjoy it if only you got back in the saddle."

The man was as stubborn as he was persuasive, and Hadley wasn't sure how to discourage him without being rude. "I assure you I wouldn't. I was pretty crazy about horses when I was young, but it no longer interests me."

"That's a shame. You were a really talented rider."

Her heart gave a little jump. "I really loved it."

"And it showed. Shannon used to complain about you all the time." Liam's intent gaze intensified his allure. "That's when I started watching you ride, and I figured out why all the other girls lost to you."

"Lolita."

"She was a big part of it, but you rode the hell out of her."

Hadley shook her head. "You said it yourself. Shannon won a lot on Lolita."

"Yeah, but her times never matched yours."

The temptation to bask in Liam's warm regard almost derailed Hadley's professionalism. The man had such a knack for making a woman feel attractive and desirable. But was he sincere? She'd labeled him a player, but maybe she'd done that to keep from being sucked in by his charm. The way he cared about Maggie made Hadley want to give him the benefit of the doubt. And yet he hadn't known he'd gotten her mother pregnant. That didn't exactly illustrate his accountability.

"Does Shannon still own her?" Parting with the mare had been one of the hardest things Hadley had ever done.

"No. She sold her after a couple years."

"How did you end up with one of her foals?"

"A client of mine in California had him."

"And Lolita?" For someone who claimed she was no longer interested in anything horse-related, Hadley was asking a lot of questions. But Lolita had been special, and she wanted to hear that the mare had ended up in a good home.

"I don't know." Her disappointment must have shown because Liam offered, "I can find out."

Hadley waved off his concern. "Oh, please don't bother. I was just…curious."

"It's no problem. Jack is a good friend."

"Really, don't trouble yourself. I'm sure she's doing great." A wave of nostalgia swept over Hadley. She wished she could say she hadn't thought about Lolita for years, but that wasn't at all the case.

Hadley didn't realize she was still holding Liam's phone until it began to ring. The image of a stunning brunette appeared on the screen. The name attached to the beautiful face: Andi. She handed Liam back his phone and rose.

"I'll take Maggie upstairs."

Andi looked like the sort of woman he'd want privacy to talk to. Hadley was halfway up the back stairs before she heard him say hello. She didn't notice the disappointment dampening her mood until she reached the nursery and settled into the rocking chair that overlooked the enormous backyard. What did she have to be down about? Of course Liam had a girlfriend. He'd always had a girlfriend, or probably several girls that he kept on ice for when he found himself with a free night.

And yet he hadn't gone out once since she'd moved into the house. He spent his evenings watching sports in the large den, laptop open, pedigrees scattered on the sofa beside him. Back when she'd been a teenager, she'd spent a fair amount of time poring over horse magazines and evaluating one stallion over another. Although it was a hobby, she liked to think her hours of study had been instrumental in how well she'd done in selecting Lolita.

Until coming to Wade Ranch, Hadley hadn't realized how much she missed everything having to do with horses. The familiar scents of the barn that clung to the jacket that Liam hung up in the entry roused emotions she'd suppressed for a long time. She missed riding. Barrel racing was in turns exhilarating and terrifying. Competing in a Western pleasure class might not be an adrenaline rush, but it presented different challenges. And no matter the outcome, a clean ride was its own reward.

Tomorrow when she took Maggie to the barn to visit Liam, she needed to keep a handle on her emotions. Liam was a persuasive salesman. He would have her butt in a saddle before she knew what was happening. Hadley shook her head, bemused and unable to comprehend why he was so determined to revive her interest in horses.

Could it be that his own passion was so strong that he wanted everyone to share in what he enjoyed? Hadley made a mental note to feel Candace out on the subject tomorrow. That settled, she picked up the book she'd been reading and settled back into the story.

A half hour later, Liam appeared in the doorway. He'd donned a warm jacket and was holding his hat.

"I have to head back to the barn. One of the yearlings got cut up in the paddock today and I need to go check on him." Liam's bright green gaze swept over her before settling on Maggie snuggled in her arms. "You two going to be okay in the house by yourselves?"

Hadley had to smile at his earnest concern. "I think we'll be fine."

"It occurs to me that I've been taking advantage of you." His words recalled their early morning encounter, and Hadley's pulse accelerated.

"How so?" she replied, as calmly as her jittery nerves allowed.

"You haven't had any time off since that first night, and I don't think you were gone more than five hours today."

"I don't mind. Maggie isn't a lot of trouble when she's sleeping, and she does a lot of that. I've been catching up on my reading. I don't have a lot of time for that when I'm in school. Although, I do have my last candle-making class at Priceless tomorrow. We're working with molds. I'd like to make it to that."

"Of course."

Almost as soon as Liam left the old Victorian, Hadley wished him back. Swaddled tight in a blanket, Maggie slept contentedly while Hadley paced from parlor to den to library to kitchen and listened to the wind howl outside. The mournful wail made her shiver, but she was too restless to snuggle on the couch in the den and let the television drown out the forlorn sounds.

Although she hadn't shared an apartment in five years, she never thought of herself as lonely. Something about living in town and knowing there was a coffee shop, library or restaurant within walking distance of her apartment was reassuring. Out here, half an hour from town, being on her own in this big old house wasn't the least bit comfortable.

Or maybe she just wanted Liam to come back.

Five

Promptly at ten o'clock the next morning, Hadley parked her SUV in front of the barn's grand entrance and shut off the engine. She'd presumed the Wade Ranch setup would be impressive, but she'd underestimated the cleverness of whoever had designed the entry. During warmer months, the grass on either side of the flagstone walkway would be a welcoming green. Large pots filled with Christmas boughs flanked the glass double doors. If Hadley hadn't been told she was about to enter a barn, she would have mistaken her destination for a showcase mansion.

Icy wind probed beneath the hem of Hadley's warm coat and pinched her cheeks when she emerged from the vehicle's warmth and fetched Maggie from the backseat. Secure in her carrier, a blanket over the retractable hood to protect her from the elements, the infant wouldn't feel the effects of the chilly air, but Hadley rushed to the barn anyway.

Slipping through the door, Hadley found herself in a forty-foot-long rectangular room with windows running the length of the space on both sides. To her right she glimpsed an indoor arena, empty at the moment. On her left, the windows overlooked a stretch of grass broken up into three paddock areas where a half-dozen horses grazed. That side of the room held a wet bar, a refrigerator and a few bar stools.

On the far end of the lounge, a brown leather couch

flanked by two matching chairs formed a seating area in front of the floor-to-ceiling fieldstone fireplace. Beside it was a doorway that Hadley guessed led to the ranch offices.

Her rubber-soled shoes made no sound on the dark wood floor, and she was glad. The room's peaked ceiling magnified even the slightest noise. She imagined when a group gathered here the volume could rattle the windows.

A woman in her early fifties appeared while Hadley was gawking at the wrought iron chandeliers. They had a Western feel without being cliché. In fact, the whole room was masculine, rugged, but at the same time had an expensive vibe that Hadley knew would appeal to a clientele accustomed to the finer things.

"Hello. You must be Hadley." The woman extended her hand and Hadley grasped it. "I'm Ivy. Liam told me you'd be coming today."

"Nice to meet you." Hadley set the baby carrier on the table in the center of the room and swept the blanket away. "And this is Maggie."

"She's beautiful." Ivy peered at the baby, who yawned expansively. "Liam talks about her nonstop."

"I imagine he does. Having her around has been a huge change for him." Hadley unfastened the straps holding the baby in the carrier and lifted her out. Maggie screwed up her face and made the cranky sounds that were a warm-up for all-out wailing. "She didn't eat very well this morning, so she's probably hungry. Would you hold her for me while I get her bottle ready?"

"I'd be happy to." Ivy didn't hesitate to snuggle Maggie despite the infant's increasing distress. "Liam has been worthless since this little one appeared on his doorstep."

Hadley had filled a bottle with premeasured powdered formula and now added warm water from the thermos she carried. "I think discovering he's a father has thrown him for a loop, but he's doing a fantastic job with Maggie."

"You think he's Maggie's father?"

Something about Ivy's neutral voice and the way she asked her question caught Hadley's attention. "Of course. Why else would Maggie's grandmother have brought her here?" She shook Maggie's bottle to mix the formula and water.

"It's not like Liam to be so careless. May I?" Ivy indicated the bottle Hadley held. "With someone as good-looking and wealthy as Liam, if he wasn't careful, a girl would have figured out how to trap him before this."

"You think Kyle is Maggie's father?"

"That would be my guess."

"But I thought he was based on the East Coast and never came home. Candace told me Maggie's mom was from San Antonio."

Hadley was uncomfortable gossiping about her employer, but reminded herself that Ivy was his family and she'd asked a direct question.

Ivy smiled down at the baby. "She's Kyle's daughter. I'm sure of it."

Any further comment Hadley might have made was forestalled by Liam's arrival. His cheeks were reddened by cold, and he carried a chill on his clothes. Hadley's pulse tripped as his penetrating gaze slid over her. The brief look was far from sexual, yet her body awakened as if he'd caressed her.

"Here are my girls," he said, stopping between Ivy and Hadley. After greeting Maggie with a knuckle to her soft cheek, he shifted his attention to Hadley. "Sorry I wasn't here to greet you, but I was delayed on a call. What do you think of the place so far?"

"Impressive." Warmth poured through her at the inconsequential brush of his arm against hers. "I never expected a ranch to have a barn like this." She indicated the stone fireplace and the windows that overlooked the arena. Staring around the large lounge kept her gaze from lingering on Liam's infectious grin and admiring the breadth of his shoulders encased in a rugged brown work jacket.

"It's been a work in progress for a while." He winked at Ivy, who rolled her eyes at him.

The obvious affection between the cousins didn't surprise Hadley. Liam had an easy charisma that tranquilized those around him. She'd wager that Liam had never once had to enforce an order he'd given. Why bully when charm got the job done faster and easier?

"I imagine a setup like this takes years to build."

"And a lot of convincing the old man," Ivy put in. "Calvin was old-school when it came to horses. He bred and sold quality horses for ranch work. And then this one came along with his love of reining and his big ideas about turning Wade Ranch into a breeding farm."

Liam tossed one of Maggie's burp rags on his shoulder and eased the infant out of Ivy's arms. "And it worked out pretty well," he said, setting the baby on his shoulder. "Come on, let's go introduce this little lady around."

With Liam leading the way through the offices, his smile broad, every inch the proud parent, he introduced Hadley to two sales associates, the breeding coordinator, the barn manager and a girl who helped Ivy three mornings a week.

Hadley expected that her role as Maggie's nanny would relegate her to the background, but Liam made her an active part of the conversation. He further startled her by bringing up her former successes at barrel racing and in the show ring. She'd forgotten how small the horse business could be when one of the salespeople, Poppy Gertz, confessed to rejoicing when Hadley had retired.

"Do you still compete?" Hadley questioned, already anticipating what the answer would be.

"Every chance I get." The brunette was in her midthirties with the steady eye and swagger of a winner. "Thinking about getting back into the game?"

At Hadley's head shake, Poppy's posture relaxed.

"We're going to get her into reining," Liam said, shifting Maggie so she faced forward.

Hadley shook her head. "I'm going to finish getting my masters and find a job as a guidance counselor." She reached out for the infant, but Liam turned away.

"Maggie and I are going to check out some horses." His easy smile was meant to lure her after them. "Why don't you join us." It was a command pitched as a suggestion.

Dutifully she did as he wanted. And in truth, it wasn't a hardship. In fact, her heartbeat increased at the opportunity to see what Wade Ranch had to offer. She'd done a little reading up about Liam and the ranch on the internet and wasn't surprised at the quality of the horses coming out of Liam's program.

They started with the stallions, since their barn was right outside the barn lounge. While Liam spoke in depth about each horse, Hadley let her thoughts drift. She'd already done her research and was far more interested in the way her body resonated with the deep, rich tone of Liam's voice. He paused in front of one stall and opened the door.

"This is WR Dakota Blue." Pride shone in Liam's voice and body language.

"He's beautiful," Hadley murmured.

The stallion stepped up to the door and nuzzled Liam's arm, nostrils flaring as he caught Maggie's scent. An infant her age couldn't clearly see objects more than eight to ten inches away, so Hadley had to wonder what Maggie made of the stallion.

"She isn't crying," Liam said as the horse lipped at Maggie's blanket. "I guess that's a good sign."

"I don't think she knows what to make of him."

"He likes her."

The stallion's gentleness and curiosity reminded her a lot of how Liam had first approached Maggie. Watching horse and owner interact with the infant, something unlocked inside Hadley. The abrupt release of the constriction left her reeling. How long had she been binding her emotions? Probably since she'd shouldered a portion of responsibility for Anna's accident.

"Hadley?" Liam's low voice brought her back to the present. He'd closed the door to the stallion's stall and stood regarding her with concern. "Is everything okay?"

"Yes. I was just thinking how lucky Maggie is to grow up in this world of horses." And she meant that with all her heart. As a kid Hadley had been such a nut about horses. She would have moved into the barn if her parents let her.

"I hope she agrees with you. My brother doesn't share my love of horses." Liam turned from the stall, and they continued down the aisle. "You miss it, don't you?"

What was the point in denying it? "I didn't think I did until I came to Wade Ranch. Horses were everything until I went off to college. I was remembering how much I missed riding and what I did to cope."

"What did you do?"

"I focused on the future, on the career I would have once I finished school."

"I'm not sure I could give up what I do."

Hadley shrugged. "You've never had to." She considered his expression as he guided her through the doors that led into the arena and wondered what it would be like to be him, to never give up something because of circumstances. "Have you ever considered what would happen if you lost Wade Ranch?"

His grin was a cocky masterpiece. "I'd start over somewhere else."

And that summed up the differences between them. Hadley let life's disappointments batter her. Liam shrugged off the hits and lived to fight another day. Which is exactly what drew her to him. She admired his confidence. His swagger. What if she hadn't let guilt overwhelm her after Anna's accident? What if she'd stood up to her parents about selling Lolita and changed her major when she realized teaching wasn't her cup of tea?

"I wish I'd gotten to know you better back when I was racing barrels," she said, letting him guide her toward a narrow wooden observation deck that ran the length of the arena.

He handed over Maggie. "You could have if you hadn't disappeared after my advice helped you win the sweepstakes. You were supposed to thank me by taking me to dinner."

"I thought you were kidding about that." Only she hadn't. She'd been thrilled that he'd wanted to go out with her. But Anna's accident had happened before she had the chance to find out if his interest in her was real. "Besides, I wasn't your type."

"What sort of type was that?"

She fussed with Maggie's sweater and didn't look at him. "Experienced."

Liam took the hit without an outward flinch. Inside he raged with frustration. "I'm not sure any woman has a worse opinion of me than you do." It was an effort to keep his voice neutral.

"My opinion isn't bad. It's realistic. And I don't know why you'd care."

Women didn't usually judge him. He was the fun guy to have around. Uncomplicated. Charming. With expensive taste and a willing attitude. But Hadley wanted more than an amiable companion who took her to spendy restaurants and exclusive clubs. Glib phrases and seduction wouldn't work on her. He'd have to demonstrate substance, and Liam wasn't sure how to go about that.

"I care because I like you." He paused a beat before adding, "And I want you to like me."

Without waiting to see her reaction, he strode across the arena toward the horse being led in by one of the grooms. He'd selected four young horses to show Hadley in the hopes of enticing her to get back in the saddle. Why it was so important to see her ride again eluded him. As always he was just going with his gut.

Liam swung up into the saddle and walked the gelding toward the raised viewing deck. "This is a Blue son. Cielo is three. I think he has a great future in reining. At the moment I personally own eight horses and I need to pare that down to five. I'm going to put him and three others through their paces, and I want you to tell me which you think I should keep and which should go."

Hadley looked appalled. "You can't ask me to do that. I'm no judge."

"When I'm done riding all four you will tell me what you think of each." He bared his teeth at her in a challenging smile. "I value your opinion."

He then spent ten minutes working Cielo through his paces all the while staying aware of Hadley's body language and expression. With Maggie asleep in her arms, Hadley had never looked so beautiful, and Liam had a hard time concentrating on his mounts. After he rode all four horses, he had a special one brought out.

"You might recognize Electric Slide from his video."

Hadley's color was high and her eyes were dancing with delight, but her smile dimmed as he approached with the colt her former mare had produced. "I can't get over how much he looks like his mother."

"Want to give him a try?"

She shook her head. "It's been too long since I've ridden, and I'm not dressed for it."

He recognized a lame excuse when he heard one. She'd worn jeans and boots to the barn and didn't want to admit the real reason for her reluctance.

"Next time." Liam swung into the saddle and pivoted the colt away.

Disappointment roared through him, unfamiliar and unpleasant. He couldn't recall the last time he'd invested so much in a project only to have it fall flat. Was that because he didn't throw himself wholly into anything, or because he rarely failed at things he did? His grandfather would say that if he was consistently successful, he wasn't challenging himself.

Isn't that why he'd quit dating a year ago and refocused on Wade Ranch? He'd grown complacent. The horse business was growing at a steady pace. He enjoyed the companionship of several beautiful women. And he was bored.

Liam's mind was only half on what he was doing as he rode Electric Slide. The pleasure had gone out of the exhibition after Hadley turned down a chance to ride. After a little while, he handed the colt off and strode across the arena toward her.

"It's almost noon," he said. "Let's go back to the house and you can tell me which horses I should keep over lunch."

"Sure."

As they ate bowls of beef stew and crusty French bread, Hadley spelled out her take on each of the horses he'd shown her.

"Cielo is a keeper. But I don't think you'd part with him no matter what anyone said to you."

"You're probably right." He missed talking horses with someone. Since his grandfather died, Liam hadn't had anyone to share his passion with. "What did you think of the bay filly?"

"Nice, but the roan mare is better, and bred to Blue you'd get a really nice foal." Hadley's gaze turned thoughtful as she stirred the stew with her spoon. "I also think you'd be fine letting the buckskin go. He's terrific, but Cielo will be a better reining horse." Her lips curved. "But I'm not telling you anything you hadn't already decided."

"I appreciate your feedback. And you're right. Of the four I showed you, I'd selected three to sell. But your suggestion that I breed Tilda to Blue was something I hadn't considered."

Her smile warmed up the already-cozy kitchen. "Glad I could help. It was fun talking horses. It was something my friends and I did all the time when I was younger. I always imagined myself living on a ranch after I finished school, breeding and training horses."

Liam's chest tightened. Hadley possessed the qualities he'd spent the last year deciding his perfect woman must have. Beautiful, loving, maternal and passionate about horses.

"Of course, that wasn't a practical dream," Hadley continued. "My parents were right to insist I put my education first. I figured that out not long after I started college."

"But what if you could have figured out a way to make it work? Start small, build something."

"Maybe ten years ago I could have." Her voice held a hint of wistfulness. A moment later, all nostalgia vanished. "These days it's no longer what I want."

Her declaration put an end to the topic. Liam held his gaze steady on her for a moment longer, wondering if he'd imagined her overselling her point. Or was he simply wishing she'd consider giving up her future plans and sticking around Royal? He'd grown attached to her in a very short period of time and wanted to see more of her. And not as his niece's nanny.

Liam pushed back from the table. "I have a meeting late this afternoon at the Texas Cattleman's Club, but I'll be back in time for you to make your class at seven."

"Thank you. I really enjoy the class as much for the company as the candle making." She carried their bowls to the sink and began rinsing them. "When I'm in school, I don't have a lot of free time."

"Sounds like you don't make enough time for fun," he said.

"I keep telling myself that I'll have plenty of time to enjoy myself once I'm done with school. In the meantime, I make the most of the free hours I have."

Liam was mulling Hadley's attitude as he strode into the Texas Cattleman's Club later that day. Originally built as a men's club around 1910, the club opened its doors to women members as well a few years ago. Liam and his grandfather had been all for the change and had even supported the addition of a child care center. For the most part, though, the decor of the original building had been left intact. The wood floors, paneled walls and hunting trophies created a decidedly masculine atmosphere.

As Liam entered the lounge and approached the bar, he overheard one table discussing the Samson Oil land purchases. This had been going on for months. Several ranchers had gone bankrupt on the heels of the destructive tornado that had swept through Royal and the surrounding ranches. Many of those who'd survived near financial ruin had then had to face the challenge of the drought that reduced lakes and creeks and made sustaining even limited herds difficult. Some without established systems of watering tanks and pumps had been forced to sell early on. Others were holding out for a miracle that wouldn't come.

"I guess I know what's on the agenda for the meeting

today," Liam mentioned as he slid into the space between his best friend, David "Mac" McCallum, and Case Baxter, current president of the Texas Cattleman's Club. "Has anybody heard what's up with all the purchases?"

Mac shook his head. "Maybe they think there are shale deposits."

"Fracking?" The man on the other side of Mac growled. "As if this damned drought isn't bad enough. What sort of poison is that process going to spill into our groundwater? I've got two thousand heads relying on well water."

Liam had heard similar complaints every time he set foot in the clubhouse. The drought was wearing on everyone. Wade Ranch relied on both wells and a spring-fed lake to keep its livestock watered. He couldn't imagine the stress of a situation where he only had one ever-dwindling source to count on.

"Mellie tells me the property lawyer who's been buying up all the land for Samson Oil quit," Case said. His fiancée's family owned several properties the oil company had tried to buy. "She's gotten friendly with one of her tenants, the woman who owns the antiques store in the Courtyard. Apparently she and Nolan Dane are involved."

"Howard Dane's son?"

"Yes, and Nolan's going back to work with him doing family law."

Liam missed who asked the question, but Case's answer got him thinking about Kyle. That his brother was still out of touch reinforced Liam's growing conviction that Maggie deserved a parent who was there for her 24/7. Obviously as long as he was on active duty, Kyle couldn't be counted on. Perhaps Liam should reach out to an attorney familiar with family law and see what his options might be for taking over custody of his niece. He made a mental note to give the man a call the next morning and set up an appointment.

"Maybe we should invite him to join the club," Liam suggested, thinking how their numbers had dwindled over the last year as more and more ranchers sold off their land.

"I think we could use some powerful allies against Samson Oil," Case said. "Nolan might not be able to give us any information on his former client, but he still has a background in property law that could be useful."

The men gathered in the bar began to move toward the boardroom where that night's meeting was to be held.

"How are things going for you at home?" Mac asked. "Is fatherhood all it's cracked up to be?"

"Maggie is not my daughter," Liam replied, wearying of everyone assuming he'd been foolhardy. "But I'm enjoying having her around. She's really quite sweet when she's not crying."

Mac laughed. "I never thought I'd see you settling down."

"A year ago I decided I wanted one good relationship rather than a dozen mediocre ones." Liam was rather impressed with how enlightened he sounded.

"And yet you've buried yourself at the ranch. How are you any closer to a good relationship when you don't get out and meet women?"

"I've heard that when you're ready, the right one comes along." An image of Hadley flashed through his mind.

Mac's hand settled forcefully on Liam's shoulder. "You're talking like an idiot. Is it sleep deprivation?"

"I have a newborn living with me. What do you think?"

But Liam knew that what was keeping him awake at night wasn't Maggie, but her nanny and the persistent hope that Waldo might sneak into Liam's bedroom and Hadley would be forced to rescue him a second time. Because if that happened, Liam had prepared a very different end to that encounter.

Six

Ivy entered Liam's office with her tablet in hand and sat down. The back of the chair thumped against the wall, and her knees bumped his desk. She growled in annoyance and rubbed her legs. Unbefitting his status as half owner of the ranch, Liam had one of the tiniest offices in the complex. He preferred to spend his days out and about and left paperwork for evenings. When he met with clients, he had an informal way of handling the meetings and usually entertained in the large lounge area or brought them into the barns.

"I'm finalizing your plans for Colorado this weekend," she said, her finger moving across the tablet screen. "The caterer is confirmed. A Suburban will be waiting for you at the airport. Give Hannah Lake a call when you land, and she will meet you at the house."

Ivy kept talking, but Liam had stopped listening. He'd forgotten all about the skiing weekend he was hosting for five of his clients. The tradition had begun several years ago. They looked forward to the event for months, and it was far too late to cancel.

"Liam?" Ivy regarded him with a steady gaze. "You seem worried. I assure you everything is ready."

"It's not that. I forgot that I was supposed to be heading to Colorado in a couple days. What am I going to do about Maggie?"

"Take her along." She jotted a note on the tablet with a stylus. "I'll see if they can set up a crib in one of the rooms."

"Have you forgotten this is supposed to be a guys' weekend? A chance for everyone to get away from their wives and families so they can smoke cigars, drink too much scotch, ski and play poker?"

"Sounds lovely." Ivy rolled her eyes.

Liam pointed at Ivy's expression. "And that is exactly what they want to get away from."

"I don't know what you're worrying about. Bring Hadley along to take care of Maggie. The house is big enough for a dozen people. No one will even know they're there."

Ivy's suggestion made sense, but Liam's instincts rebelled at her assumption that no one would realize they were present. He would know. Just like every other night when she slept down the hall.

"That's true enough, and Maggie is doing better at night. She barely fusses at all before going back to sleep." Liam wondered how much of a fight Hadley would make about flying to Colorado. He got to his feet. It was late enough in the afternoon for him to knock off. He'd been looking forward to spending a little time with Maggie before dinner. "I'd better give Hadley a heads-up."

"Let me know if she has anything special to arrange for Maggie." With that, Ivy exited the office.

Liam scooped his hat off the desk and settled it on his head. As he drove the ten minutes between barns and house, Liam considered the arguments for and against taking Maggie with him to Colorado. In the ten days since his niece had become a part of his life, he'd grown very attached to her. When his brother contacted him, Liam intended to convince him to give the baby up. With the dangerous line of work his brother was in, Maggie would be better off with the sort of stable home environment found here on Wade Ranch.

Liam entered the house and followed the scent of wood smoke to the den. Hadley looked up from her book as Liam entered. "You're home early."

"I came home to spend some time with Maggie." And with her. Had he imagined the way her eyes had lit up upon seeing him? They'd spent a great deal of time together in the last few days. All under the guise of caring for Maggie, but Liam knew his own motives weren't as pure as he'd let on.

"She had a rough afternoon."

She glanced down at the sleeping infant nestled in her arms. Hadley's fond expression hit Liam in the gut.

"She looks peaceful now."

"I only got her to sleep half an hour ago." Hadley began shifting the baby in her arms. "Do you want to hold her?"

"Not yet. I spent most of the day in the saddle. I'm going to grab a shower first."

He rushed through his cleanup and ran a comb through his damp hair. Dressed in brown corduroy pants and a denim shirt, he headed back to the den. The afternoon light had faded until it was too dark for Hadley to read, but instead of turning on the lamps, she was relying on the flickering glow of the fire. Outside, the wind howled, and she shivered.

"Is it as chilly as it sounds?"

"I suspect the windchill will be below freezing tonight."

He eased down on the couch beside her and took the baby. Their bodies pressed against each other hip to knee during the exchange, and Liam smiled as her scent tickled his nose. They'd become a well-oiled machine in the last few days, trading off Maggie's care like a couple in sync with each other and their child's needs. It had given him a glimpse of what life would be like with a family. Liam enjoyed Hadley's undemanding company. She'd demonstrated an impish sense of humor when sharing stories of her fellow nannies' adventures in caretaking, and he was wearing down her resistance to talking about horses by sharing tales of people she used to compete against.

"I have a business trip scheduled in a couple days," Liam began, eyeing Hadley as he spoke. Her gaze was on the baby in his arms.

"How long will you be gone?"

"I rented a house in Colorado for a week, but usually I'm only gone for four days." He paused, thinking how he'd prefer to stay in this cozy triangle with Hadley and Maggie rather than flying off to entertain a group of men. "It's a ski weekend for five of my best clients."

"Are you worried about leaving Maggie here?"

"Yes. I want to bring her along." He paused a beat before adding, "I want you to come, as well." He saw the arguments building in her blue eyes. He already had the answer to her first one. "Candace has offered to take Waldo, so you don't have to worry about him."

"I've never traveled with a client before." She wasn't demonstrating the resistance he'd expected. "Are you sure there will be room for us?"

"The house is quite large. There are seven bedrooms. Ivy is coordinating the trip and said you should let her know about anything you think Maggie might need. She is already making arrangements for a crib."

"When would we leave?"

"We'll fly up in two days. I like to get in a day early to make sure everything is in place. Is that enough time for you to get what you'll need?"

"Sure." But she was frowning as she said it.

"Is something wrong?"

She laughed self-consciously. "I've never seen snow before. What will I need to buy besides a warm coat?"

"You've never seen snow?" Liam was excited at the

thought of being there when Hadley experienced the beauty of a winter day in the mountains.

"For someone as well traveled as you are, that must seem pretty unsophisticated."

Liam considered her comment. "You said you'd never traveled with your clients. Is that because you didn't want to?"

"It's mostly been due to school and timing. I always figured there'd be plenty of time to travel after I graduated and settled into a job with regular hours and paid vacation time."

Her wistful smile gave him some notion of how long and arduous a journey it had been toward finishing her master's degree.

He felt a little hesitant to ask his next question. "Have you flown in a small plane before?"

"No." She drew the word out, her gaze finding and holding his. Anxiety and eagerness pulled at the corners of her mouth. "How small is small?"

Small turned out to be forty feet in length with a forty-three-foot wingspan. Hadley's heart gave a little bump as she approached the elegant six-seat jet with three tiny oval windows. She didn't know what she'd been expecting, maybe a single-prop plane with fixed wheels like the ones used by desperate movie heroes to escape or chase bad guys.

"This doesn't look so scary, does it?" She whispered the question to a sleepy Maggie.

Hadley stopped at the steps leading up to the plane. Liam had gone ahead with her luggage and overnight bag carrying all of Maggie's things. Now he emerged from the plane and reached down to take Maggie's carrier.

"Come on in." Liam's irresistible grin pulled Hadley forward.

She almost floated up the stairs. His charm banished her nervousness, allowing her to focus only on the excitement of visiting Colorado for the first time. Not that she'd see much of it. Her job was to take care of Maggie. But even to glimpse the town of Vail covered in snow as they drove past would be thrill enough.

The plane's interior was luxurious, with room enough for a pilot and five passengers. There were six beige leather seats, two facing forward and two backward as well as the two in the cockpit. She knew nothing about aviation equipment, but the instrument panel placed in front of the pilot and copilot seats had three large screens filled with data as well as an abundance of switches and buttons and looked very sophisticated.

"I set up Maggie's car seat here because I thought you'd prefer to face forward. You'll find bottles of water and ice over there." He pointed to the narrow cabinet behind the cockpit. "There's also a thermos of hot water to make Maggie's bottle."

"Thank you. I made one before we left because it helps babies to adjust to altitudes if they're sucking on something."

"Great. We should be set then."

Hadley settled into her seat and buckled herself in. She looked up in time to see Liam closing the airplane's door.

"Wait," she called. "What about the pilot?"

The grin he turned on her was wolfish. "I am the pilot." With a wink, he slid into the left cockpit seat and began going through a preflight check.

Surprise held her immobile for several minutes before her skin heated and her breath rushed out. For almost two weeks now his actions and the things he'd revealed about himself kept knocking askew her preconceived notions about him. It was distracting. And dangerous.

To avoid fretting over her deepening attraction to Liam,

Hadley pulled out Maggie's bottle and a bib. As the plane taxied she had a hard time ignoring the man at the controls, and surrendered to the anxiety rising in her.

What was she doing? Falling for Liam was a stupid thing to do. The man charmed everyone without even trying.

As the plane lifted off, her stomach dipped and her adrenaline surged. Hadley offered Maggie the bottle and the infant sucked greedily at it. Out the window, land fell away, and the small craft bounced a little on the air currents. To keep her nervousness at bay, Hadley focused all her attention on Maggie. The baby was not the least bit disturbed by the plane's movements. In fact, her eyes were wide and staring as if it was one big adventure.

After what felt like an endless climb, the plane leveled off. Hadley freed Maggie from her car seat so she could burp her. Peering out the window, she saw nothing but clouds below them. With Liam occupied in the cockpit and Maggie falling asleep in her arms, Hadley let her thoughts roam free.

Several hours later, after Liam landed the plane at a small airport outside Vail, their rental car sped toward their destination. When she'd stepped off the plane, Hadley had been disappointed to discover that very little snow covered the ground. She'd imagined that in the middle of January there would be piles and piles of the white stuff everywhere she looked. But now, as they neared the mountains, her excitement began to build once more.

Framed against an ice-blue sky, the snow-covered peaks surrounding the town of Vail seemed impossibly high. But she could see the ski runs that started near the summit and carved through the pine-covered face of each mountain. Liam drove the winding roads without checking the navigation, obviously knowing where he was headed.

"What do you think?"

"It's beautiful."

"Wait until you see the views from the house. They're incredible."

"Do you rent this house every year?"

"A longtime friend of my grandfather owns it."

"I didn't realize you like to ski."

"I had a lot more free time when I was younger, but these days I try to get out a couple times a year. I go to New Mexico when I can get away for a weekend because it's close."

"It must be nice having your own plane so you can take off whenever you want."

"I'm afraid it's been pretty idle lately. I've spent almost ninety percent of my time at the ranch this year."

And the other ten percent meeting Maggie's mother and spending the night with her. Hadley glanced into the backseat where the baby was batting at one of the toys clipped to her car seat.

"You said that's been good for your business," Hadley said, "but don't you miss showing?"

"All the time."

"So why'd you give it up?" From the way Liam's expression turned to stone, she could tell her question had touched on something distasteful. "I'm sorry. I didn't mean to pry. Forget I said anything."

"No, it's okay. A lot of people have asked me that question. I'll tell you what I tell them. After my grandfather died, I discovered how much time it takes to run Wade Ranch."

She suspected that was only half of the reason, but she didn't pry anymore. "Any chance your brother, Kyle, will come back to Texas to help you?"

"No." Liam's answer was a clipped single syllable and discouraged further questions. "I'm finding a balance between ranch business as a whole and the horse side that I love. Last summer I hired a sales manager for the cattle division. I think you met Emma Jane. She's been a terrific asset."

She *had* terrific assets, Hadley thought wryly. The beautiful blonde was memorable for many reasons, not the least of which was the way her eyes and her body language communicated her interest in Liam. That he'd seemed oblivious had surprised Hadley. Since when did a man who enjoyed having beautiful women around not notice one right beneath his nose?

Maybe becoming a father had affected him more than Hadley had given him credit for.

Liam continued, "But it's not like having someone I could put in charge of the entire operation."

Obviously Liam was stretched thin. Maybe that's why he'd been looking so lighthearted these last few days. The break from responsibility would do him good.

Forty minutes after they'd left the airport, Liam drove up a steep driveway and approached a sprawling home right at the base of the mountain.

"We're staying here?" Hadley gawked at the enormous house.

"I told you there was enough room for you and Maggie." He stopped the SUV beside a truck and shot her a broad smile. "Let's get settled in and then head into town for dinner. It's a quarter mile walk if you think Maggie would be okay."

"We can bundle her up. The fresh air sounds lovely." The temperature hovered just above freezing, but it was sunny and there wasn't any wind, so Hadley was comfortable in her brand-new ski jacket and winter boots.

A tall man in his midsixties with an athletic bounce to his stride emerged from the house and headed straight for Liam. "Mr. Wade, how good to have you with us again."

"Hello, Ben." The two men shook hands, and Liam turned to gesture to Hadley, who'd unfastened Maggie from her car seat and now walked around to the driver's side. "This is Ms. Stratton and Maggie."

"Ivy mentioned you were bringing family with you this year. How nice."

The vague reference to family disturbed Hadley. Why couldn't Liam just admit that he had a daughter? He obviously loved Maggie. What blocked him from acknowledging her as his? This flaw in his character bothered Hadley more than it should. But it was none of her business. And it wasn't fair that she expected more of him. Liam was her employer. She had no right to judge.

"Nice to meet you, Ben," she said.

While Liam and Ben emptied the SUV of luggage and ski equipment, Hadley carried Maggie inside and passed through the two-story foyer to the large living room. The whole front of the house that faced the mountain was made up of tall windows.

"There's a nice room upstairs for you and Maggie." Liam came over to where she stood staring at the mountain range. "Ben said he was able to get a crib set up in there."

Hadley followed Liam up a broad staircase. At the top he turned right. The home sprawled across the hillside, providing each bedroom with a fantastic view. The room Hadley and Maggie were to share was at the back of the house and looked west, offering views of both mountains and the town. At four in the afternoon, the sun was sliding toward the horizon, gilding the snow.

"Is this okay?"

"It's amazing." The room was large by Hadley's standards, but she guessed it was probably the smallest the house offered. Still, it boasted a queen-size bed, plush seating for two before the enormous picture window and a stone fireplace that took up most of the wall the bed faced. The crib had been set up in the corner nearest to the door that led to the hall.

"I'm next door in case you need me."

Her nerves trumpeted a warning at his proximity. Not that there was any cause for alarm. She and Liam had been sleeping down the hall from each other for almost two weeks.

Plus, it wasn't as though they would be alone. Tomorrow, five others would be joining them, and from the way Liam described past years, the men would be occupied with cards, drinking and conversation late into the night.

"What time should I be ready to leave for dinner?"

"I think we won't want to have Maggie out late. What if we leave here in an hour?"

"I'll have both of us ready."

With Maggie snug in her new winter clothes and Hadley dressed for the cold night air in a turtleneck sweater and black cords, they came downstairs to find Liam waiting in the entry. He held Hadley's insulated jacket while she slid her feet into warm boots and then helped her into the coat. The brush of his knuckles against her shoulders caused butterflies to dance in her stomach. The longing to lean backward against his strong chest was so poignant, Hadley stopped breathing.

Because she'd had her back to him, Liam had no idea how the simple act of chivalry had rocked her equilibrium. Thank goodness she'd learned to master her facial expressions during her last five years of being a nanny. By the time Liam picked up Maggie's carrier, set his hand on the front door latch and turned an expectant gaze upon her, she was ready to offer him a polite smile.

Liam closed and locked the door behind them and then offered his arm to help Hadley negotiate the driveway's steep slope.

"You have Maggie," she told him, considering how lovely it would be to snuggle against his side during the half-mile walk. "Don't worry about me." She might have convinced him if her boots hadn't picked that second to skid on an icy patch.

"I think I can handle a girl on each arm," he said, his voice rich with laughter.

Hadley slipped her arm through Liam's and let him draw her close. The supporting strength of his muscular arm was supposed to steady her, not weaken her knees, but Hadley couldn't prevent her body from reveling in her escort's irresistible masculinity.

At the bottom of the driveway, Hadley expected Liam to release her, but he showed no inclination to set her free. Their boots crunched against the snow-covered pavement as they headed toward town. Sunset was still a little ways off, but clouds had moved in to blanket the sky and speed up the shift to evening. With her heart hammering a distracting tattoo against Hadley's breastbone, she was at a loss for conversation. Liam seemed okay with the silence as he walked beside her.

The restaurant Liam chose was a cute bistro in the heart of Vail Village. "It's my favorite place to eat when I come here," he explained, holding open the door and gesturing her inside.

The early hour meant the tables were only a third full. The hostess led them to a cozy corner table beside the windows that ran along the street front and offered a wonderful view of the trees adorned with white lights. Above their heads, small halogen lights hung from a rustic beam ceiling. A double-sided stone fireplace split the large room into two cozy spaces. White table linens, candlelight and crystal goblets etched with the restaurant's logo added to the romantic ambience.

"I hope the food is half as good as the decor," Hadley commented, bending over Maggie's carrier to remove the infant from her warm nest before she overheated.

"I assure you it's much better. Chef Mongillo is a culinary genius."

Since becoming Maggie's nanny, Hadley had grown accustomed to the rugged rancher Liam was at home and forgot that his alter ego was sophisticated and well traveled. And by extension, his preferred choice of female companionship was worldly and stylish. This abrupt return to reality jarred her out of her dreamy mood, and she chastised herself for forgetting her role in Liam's life.

Taking refuge behind the tall menu, she scanned the delicious selection of entrees and settled on an ahi tuna dish with artichoke, black radish and egg confit potato. The description made her mouth water. Liam suggested the blue crab appetizer and ordered a bottle of sauvignon blanc to accompany it.

She considered the wisdom of drinking while on duty, but deliberated only a few seconds before her first sip. The crisp white burst on her taste buds and her gaze sought Liam. The glint lighting his eyes was a cross between amusement and appreciation. Heat collected in her cheeks and spread downward.

She spoke to distract herself from the longing his scrutiny awakened. "This is delicious."

"Glad you like it." His deep voice pierced her chest and spurred her heart to race. "I'm really glad you were willing to come along this weekend."

This is not a date.

"Are you kidding? You had me at snow." She tried to sound lighthearted and casual, but ended up coming across breathless and silly. Embarrassed, she glanced away. The view out the window seemed the best place for her attention. What she saw made her catch her breath. "And speaking of snow..."

Enormous white flakes drifted past the window. It was

so thick that it was almost impossible to see the storefronts across the cobblestoned street.

"It's really beautiful. I can see why you come here."

"I arranged the weather just for you." As lines went, it wasn't original, but it made her laugh.

Hadley slanted a wry glance his way. "That was very nice of you."

"And I'm sure the guys will be happy to have fresh powder to ski."

When the waiter brought their appetizer, Liam asked about the weather. "How many inches are you expecting?"

"I've heard anywhere from eight to twelve inches here. More elsewhere. It's a pretty huge system moving across the Midwest."

"That's not going to be good for people trying to get in or out of here."

"No. From what I've heard, the Denver airport is expecting to cancel most if not all of their flights tomorrow. I don't know about Eagle County." Which was where they'd landed a few hours earlier.

"Sounds like we're going to be snowed in," Liam said, not appearing particularly concerned.

Hadley didn't share his nonchalance. "What does that mean for your guests?"

"I'll have to check in with them tonight. They might be delayed for a couple days or decide to cancel altogether depending on how long the storm persists."

"But…" What did she plan to say? If the storm moving in made inbound travel impossible, they certainly couldn't fly out. Which meant she, Maggie and Liam were going to be stuck in Vail for the foreseeable future. Alone.

Hadley focused on the food in front of her, annoyed by her heart's irregular beat. What did she think was going to happen in the next few days? Obviously her hormones thought she and Liam would engage in some sort of passionate affair.

The idiocy of the notion made her smile.

Seven

Liam knew he'd concealed his delight at being snowed in with Hadley, so why was she so distracted all of a sudden? And what was with the smile that curved her luscious lips?

He cleared his throat to alleviate the sudden tightness. "I take it you like blue crab?"

Hadley glanced up, and her eyes widened as she met his gaze. "Yes. It's delicious." Her attention strayed toward the window and the swiftly falling flakes. "It's really magical."

Her dreamy expression startled him. He'd become accustomed to her practicality and was excited that her professional mask might be slipping.

With the snow piling up outside, they didn't linger over dinner. As much as Liam would have enjoyed several more hours of gazing into her eyes and telling stories that made her laugh, they needed to get Maggie home and tucked in for the night. His disappointment faded as he considered that they could continue the conversation side by side on the living room sofa. Without the barrier of a table between them, things could get interesting.

"Ready?" he asked, as he settled the check and stood.

"Sure."

Helping her into her coat gave him the excuse to move close enough to inhale her scent and give her shoulders a friendly squeeze. He hoped he hadn't imagined the slight hitch of her breath as he touched her.

Liam gestured for Hadley to go ahead of him out of the restaurant. They retraced their steps through town, navigating the slippery sidewalk past trees strung with white lights and shop windows displaying their wares. Liam insisted Hadley take his arm. He'd enjoyed the feel of her snuggled against him during the walk into town.

Once the commercial center of the town was behind them, the mountain once again dominated the view. As they strolled along, boots sinking into an inch of fresh snow, Liam was convinced he couldn't have planned a more romantic walk home. The gently falling snow captured them in a world all their own, isolating them from obligations and interruptions.

Hadley laughed in delight as fat flakes melted on her cheeks and eyelashes. He wanted to kiss each one away and had a hard time resisting the urge to take her in his arms to do just that. If not for the weight of Maggie's carrier in his hand, he doubted if he could have resisted.

The strength of his desire for Hadley gave him pause. It wasn't just sexual attraction, although heaven knew his lust flared every time she came within arm's reach. No, it was something more profound that made him want her. The way she took care of Maggie, not as if she was being paid to look after her but with affection and genuine concern for her welfare.

He could picture them as partners in the ranch. She had a great eye when it came to seeing the potential in horses, and he had no doubt if she would just remember how much she enjoyed her days of showing that she would relish being involved with the ranch's future.

Yet she'd demonstrated complete disinterest in the horses, and he had yet to figure out why, when it was obviously something she'd been passionate about ten years earlier. Maybe he should accept that she was planning to leave Royal after she graduated. Plus, she'd invested five years getting a graduate degree in guidance counseling. Would she be willing to put that aside?

"You're awfully quiet all of a sudden," Hadley commented. "Cat got your tongue?"

He snorted at her. "I was just thinking about the girl I met ten years ago."

"Which one? There must have been hundreds." An undercurrent of insecurity ran beneath her teasing.

Liam decided to play it straight. "The only one that got away."

His declaration was met with silence, and for a moment the companionable mood between them grew taut with anticipation. He walked on, curious how she'd respond.

"You can't really mean me," she said at last. "You must have met dozens of girls who interested you where the circumstances or the timing weren't right."

"Probably. But only one sticks out in my mind. You. I truly regret never getting a chance to know you better."

While she absorbed this, they reached the driveway of the house where they were staying and began to climb. In minutes he was going to lose her to Maggie's bedtime ritual.

"Why did you sell Lolita and disappear?"

She tensed at his question. "You asked me before why I was no longer interested in horses. It's the same reason I stopped showing. At that sweepstakes show, my best friend fell during her run. She wanted really badly to beat me, so she pushed too hard and her horse lost his footing. He went down with her under him. She broke her back and was paralyzed."

"I remember hearing that someone had been hurt, but I didn't realize how serious it was."

"After that I just couldn't race anymore. It was my fault that she rode the way she did. If I hadn't… She really wanted to beat me." Hadley let out a shaky sigh. "After it happened she refused to talk to me or see me."

Liam sensed there was more to the story he wasn't getting, but didn't want to push deeper into a sensitive issue. "I don't want to downplay your guilt over what was obviously a tragedy, but don't you think it's time you forgave yourself for what happened?"

Hadley gave a bitter laugh. "My best friend is constantly getting on my case for not letting go of mistakes I've made in the past. She's more of a learn-something-and-move-on sort of a girl."

"Maybe if you start riding again you could put it behind you?"

"I'll think about it."

Which sounded like a big fat *no* to Liam's ears. As soon as they entered the front door, Hadley took Maggie's carrier.

"Thank you for dinner."

"You're welcome."

"I'd better get this one into bed." She paused as if having more to say.

"It's still early. I'm going to bet there's some seriously decadent desserts in the kitchen. Ivy knows my guest John Barr has quite a sweet tooth, and she always makes sure it's satisfied."

"It's been a long day, and I'm dying to finish the mystery I started on the plane. I'll see you in the morning."

Liam watched her ascend the stairs and considered following, but decided if she refused to have dessert with him, she was probably not in the mood for his company. He'd ruined what had been a promising evening by asking about matters that were still painful to her. Well, he'd wanted to get to know her better, and he'd succeeded in that.

Pouring himself a scotch, Liam sat down in front of the enormous television and turned on a hockey game. As he watched the players move about the rink, his thoughts ran to the woman upstairs. Getting to know her was not going to be without its ups and downs. She was complicated and enigmatic.

But Liam hadn't won all his reining titles because he lacked finesse and patience. He thrived on the challenge of figuring out what each horse needed to excel. No reason he couldn't put those same talents to use with Hadley.

He intended to figure out what this filly was all about, and if he was lucky—the news reports were already talking about airport shutdowns all over the Midwest—it looked as though he'd have four uninterrupted days and nights to do so.

After a restless night pondering how some inexplicable thing had changed in her interaction with Liam, Hadley got up early and went to explore the gourmet kitchen. Up until last night she'd characterized her relationship with him as boss and employee. Maybe it had grown to friendship of a sort. They enjoyed each other's company, but except for that time she'd gone to retrieve Waldo from his bedroom— which didn't count—he'd never given her any indication that the physical desire she felt for him was reciprocal.

Because of that, Hadley had been confident she could come on this trip and keep Liam from seeing her growing attraction for him. That was before they'd had a romantic dinner together and then walked home in the snow. Now a major storm system had stalled over the Midwest, stranding them alone in this snowy paradise, and she was in trouble.

"I'm sorry your clients won't make the skiing weekend," she said, her gaze glued to the pan of bacon she was fixing. Nearby a carton of eggs sat on the granite counter; she was making omelets.

"I'm not." Liam's deep voice sounded far too close behind her for comfort. "I'm actually looking forward to spending the time with you."

She should ignore the lure of his words and the invitation she'd glimpsed in his eyes the night before. Hadn't she learned her lesson with Noah? Getting emotionally involved with clients was never smart. She couldn't lie to herself and pretend the only thing she felt for Liam was sexual attraction. Granted, there was a great deal of lust interfering with her clear thinking, but she wasn't the type to lose her mind over a hot guy.

What Liam inspired in her was a complicated mixture of physical desire, admiration and wariness. The last was due to how she wanted to trust his word when he claimed he wasn't Maggie's father. Obviously the man had a knack for making women come around to his point of view. She was back to pondering his apparent sincerity and her susceptibility. What other outrageous lie could he tell her that she would believe?

Liam had propped his hip against the counter beside her and was watching her through narrowed eyes. "What can I help you with?"

"You never offer to help Candace." The statement came out sounding like an accusation.

"I've given up trying. Haven't you noticed she doesn't like anyone interfering in her kitchen?" He reached across her to snag a piece of cooked bacon off the plate where it cooled. His gaze snagged hers as he broke the piece in half and offered part to her. "I'm completely at your disposal. What would you like me to do?"

Hadley told herself there was no subtext beneath his question, but her body had a completely different interpretation. She wanted to turn off the stove and find a use for the kitchen that had nothing to do with cooking.

"I'm going to make omelets. Can you get the ingredients you want in yours from the fridge?"

Liam's lazy smile suggested that he'd heard the uneven-ness of her tone and had an idea he'd put it there. But he didn't push his advantage. Instead, he did as she asked, and Hadley was left with space to breathe and a moment to cool off. Almost immediately she discovered how this had back-fired. The gap between them didn't bring relief from her cravings, but increased her longing for him. She was in a great deal of trouble.

Without asking, he pulled out a cutting board and began chopping onion and tomatoes. Engrossed in the task, he didn't notice her stare. Or that's what she thought until he spoke.

"Candace doesn't work 24/7," he commented, setting a second pan on the six-burner stove and adding olive oil. "I have been known to cook for myself from time to time."

"Sorry for misjudging you."

"You do that a lot."

"Apologize?"

"Jump to negative conclusions about me."

"That's not true."

"Isn't it?" He dumped the diced onions into the pan and stirred them. "From the moment you walked into my house you pegged me as a womanizing jerk who slept with some random woman, got her pregnant and never contacted her again."

She couldn't deny his statement. "I don't think you're a jerk."

"But you think I treat women like playthings."

"It's none of my business what you do."

Liam's breath gusted out. "For the rest of this trip I give you a pass to speak your mind with me. I'm not going to dance around topics while you keep the truth bottled up."

"Fine." Hadley couldn't understand why she was so an-noyed all of a sudden. "Back when I used to show, you had a reputation for going through girls like chewing gum."

"Sure, I dated a lot, and I know that not every girl was happy when I broke things off, but I never treated any of them like they were disposable."

"What do you call sleeping with them once and then never calling again?"

"I never did that. Who said I did?"

"A friend of mine knew someone..." Hadley trailed off. Why hadn't she ever questioned whether what Anna had said about him was true?

Anger faded from Liam's green eyes. "And because she was your friend, you believed her."

Liam shook his head and went back to stirring the onions. While Hadley searched for answers in his expression, he added raw spinach to the pan and set a lid on it.

"We have cheddar and Cojack cheese," Liam said. "Which would you prefer?"

"Cojack." Hadley had finished with the bacon while they'd been talking and began cracking eggs for their omelets. She moved mechanically, burdened by the notion that she'd done Liam a great injustice. "I'll pour some orange juice. Do you want toast? There's some honey wheat that looks good."

"That's fine. I'll finish up the omelets." His neutral tone gave away none of his thoughts, but Hadley moved around the large kitchen with the sense that she was in the wrong.

Instead of eating in the formal dining room, Hadley set the small kitchen table. She paused to stare out the window at the new blanket of snow covering the mountains and gave a small thank-you to the weather gods for giving her and Liam this weekend alone. He was a far more complicated man than she'd given him credit for, and she welcomed the opportunity to get inside his head between now and when they returned to Royal.

A few minutes later, Hadley carried Maggie's carrier to the table and Liam followed her with plates of omelets and the bacon. Awkward silence had replaced their companionable chatter from the previous evening. It was her fault. She'd wounded him with Anna's tale. But whom was she supposed to believe? Her best friend at the time or a man who admitted to *dating* a lot of women?

The delicious omelet was like a mouthful of sand. Hadley washed the bite down with orange juice and wondered what she was supposed to believe. For ten years she'd lived with guilt over the pain her actions had caused Anna. What if none of it had been as her friend said?

"I know you haven't had any reason to believe I've left my playboy ways behind me," Liam began, his own food untouched. "And perhaps I deserve your skepticism, but I'd like to point out that nothing has happened between you and me, despite my strong attraction to you."

"Strong...attraction?" Hadley fumbled out the words, her heart hammering hard against her ribs.

His gaze was direct and intense as he regarded her. "Very. Strong."

What could she say to that? She looked to Maggie for help, but the baby had her attention locked on the string of stuffed bugs strapped to the handle of her carrier and was too content to provide a convenient distraction.

"I wish you weren't," she said at last, the statement allowing her to retreat from a very dangerous precipice.

"That makes two of us. And I have no intention of worsening your opinion of me by doing anything that makes you uncomfortable. I wouldn't bring it up at all except that I wanted to illustrate that I'm done with casual relationships." He picked up his fork and began breaking up his omelet.

"When you say casual relationships..."

"Ones that are primarily sexual in nature." His head bobbed in a decisive nod.

"So you're not…"

"Having sex? No." He gave her a rueful grin. "I haven't been with anyone in a year."

That wasn't possible. "But Maggie…"

"Isn't mine. She's my brother's daughter."

Hadley stared at him, saw that this wasn't a come-on or a ploy. He was completely serious. And she wanted to believe him. Because if he hadn't been with anyone in a year, that meant he might not be the player she'd taken him for. Suddenly, the speed at which she was falling for him was a little less scary than it had been five minutes ago.

"Why haven't you…?"

He took pity on her and answered her half-asked question. "When Grandfather died and I inherited half of Wade Ranch, it suddenly became apparent that the women I'd been involved with saw me as a good time and nothing more."

"And you wanted to be more?" She couldn't imagine Liam being anything less than completely satisfied with who he was, and this glimpse into his doubts made him more interesting than ever.

"Not to be taken seriously bothered me a great deal."

Hadley was starting to see his problem. "Maybe it was just the women in your sphere who felt that way. If you found some serious women, maybe then you'd be taken seriously."

"You're a serious woman." His green eyes hardened. "And you've been giving me back-off vibes from the moment we met."

"But that's because I work for you and what sort of professional would I be if I let myself get involved with my employer?" *Again*. She clung to the final thought. This conversation had strayed too deep into personal territory.

"You won't be working for me forever. What happens then? Does a serious girl like you give me a chance?"

* * *

Liam watched Hadley's face for some sign of her thoughts. Sharing the details of his recent personal crisis had been a risk. She could decide he was playing her. Building up sympathy to wear down her defenses. Or she might write him off as a sentimental fool in desperate need of a strong woman. The thought of that amused him.

"I...don't know."

He refused to be disappointed by her answer. "Then obviously I have my work cut out for me."

"What does that mean?"

"You need to be convinced I'm sincere. I'm up for the challenge."

"Is that what you think? That I need to be convinced I'm wrong about you?" She shook her head in disgust. "I can make up my own mind, thank you."

Torn between admiration and frustration, Liam debated his next words. "I seem to be saying everything wrong today." To his amazement, she smiled.

"I might be harder on you than you deserve. It's really not for me to offer an opinion on your past behavior or judge the decisions you've made." She glanced at Maggie and then fastened serious blue eyes on him. "You're wonderful with Maggie, and that's the man I'd like to get to know better."

In business and horses, this would be the sort of breakthrough he'd capitalize on. But her next words deflated his optimism.

"Unfortunately, you are also my boss, and that's a line I can't cross."

But she wanted to. He recognized regret in her downcast eyes and the tight line of her lips. With the snow still falling, he would have plenty of time to turn her to his way of thinking. The chemistry between them was worth exploring. As were the emotions she roused in him. She wouldn't react well to being rushed, but it appeared he'd have several days with which to nudge her along.

"Any idea how you'd like to spend the day?" he asked. "It's unlikely we'll be dug out any time soon,"

She gestured to the mountain. "I thought you'd be dying to go skiing. Isn't all this new powder a skier's dream?"

How to explain his reluctance to leave her behind? "It's not as much fun alone."

"That makes sense." But her expression didn't match her words.

"You don't look convinced."

"You've never struck me as a man who sits still for long. I can't imagine you'll be happier here than out on the slopes."

"Are you trying to get rid of me for some reason?"

"No. Nothing like that."

"I don't want to leave you and Maggie alone."

"We'd have been alone if your guests showed up. No reason anything has to be different."

Except that it was. This was no longer a business trip. It had morphed into a vacation. And Liam had very different expectations for how he'd like to spend his time.

That night's dinner had been arranged for six, but since it was beef medallions in a red wine sauce with mushrooms, herb-roasted potatoes and creamed spinach, it had been a simple matter for the chef to make only two portions.

With the chandelier lights dimmed and flickering candlelight setting a romantic scene, the tension kept rising between them. Liam had dated enough women to recognize when a woman was attracted to him, but he'd never known one as miserable about it as Hadley.

"You are obviously uncomfortable about something," he commented, breaking the silence that had grown heavier since the chef had presented them with dessert and left for the night.

"Why would you say that?"

"Because you are as jumpy as a filly being stalked by a mountain lion."

Her brows drew together. "That's ridiculous."

"What's on your mind?" he persisted, ignoring her protest. When she pressed her lips together and shook her head, he decided to talk for her. "Let me guess. Since you started acting all skittish shortly after learning we were going to be snowed in alone together, you think I'm going to seduce you." Liam sipped his wine and observed her reaction.

"I don't think that."

He could see that was true. So what gave her cause for concern? "Oh," he drew the word out, "then you're worried you're going to try to seduce me."

One corner of her mouth lifted in a self-deprecating grin. "As if I could do that." She had visibly relaxed thanks to his bluntness.

"You aren't giving yourself enough credit."

She rolled her eyes, but refrained from arguing. "I thought you'd given up casual sex."

"I have. Which should make you feel more relaxed about our circumstances." He set his elbows on the table and leaned forward.

"Okay, maybe I'm a little on edge."

"What can I do to put you at ease?"

"Nothing. It's my problem."

"But I don't want there to be a problem."

"You really aren't going to let this go, are you?"

He shook his head. "What if I promise that whatever you say will not be held against you after we leave here?" He spread his arms wide. "Go ahead, give me your best shot."

"It's awkward and embarrassing."

She paused as if hoping he'd jump in and reassure her again. Liam held his tongue and tapped his chest to remind her he could take whatever she had to dish out.

"I'm attracted to you, and that's making me uncomfortable, because you're my boss and I shouldn't be having those sorts of feelings for you."

He'd been expecting something along those lines and wished she wasn't so damned miserable about feeling that way. "See, that wasn't so hard. I like you. You like me."

"And nothing can happen between us."

"If that's what you really want." If that was the case, he would respect her decision. But nothing would convince him to like it.

"It is." Her expression closed down. "I made a mistake once, and I promised myself I'd never do anything like that ever again."

"You are too hard on yourself. Everyone screws up. You shouldn't beat yourself up about it."

"That's what my best friend tells me."

"Sounds like a smart friend." Liam dropped the subject. Asking her to confide in him would only cause her to shut down, and he didn't want that to happen. "What should we do after dinner? We could watch a movie. Or there's board games stored in the front closet if you think you can best me at Monopoly or backgammon."

"You don't really want to play either of those, do you?"

"Not really."

"I suppose if you were entertaining clients, you'd go out to a bar, or if you didn't have the energy for that after a full day of skiing, you'd sit around drinking scotch and smoking cigars."

"Something like that." Neither of those activities sounded like much fun while his thoughts were filled with Hadley's soft lips yielding beneath his and the wonders of her generous curves pressed against his body. Gripped by a fit of restlessness, Liam pushed back from the table. "You know, I think I'll head into town and grab a drink. Don't wait up. It'll probably be a late night. I'll see you tomorrow."

Eight

Hadley sat in miserable silence for several minutes after the front door closed behind Liam, cursing her decision to push him away. Was it fair that doing the right thing made her unhappy? Shouldn't she be feeling wretched only after acting against her principles?

With a disgusted snort, Hadley cleared the dessert dishes from the table and set them in the sink. With a lonely evening stretched out before her, she puttered in the kitchen, washing the plates and wineglasses, wiping down the already-immaculate counters and unloading the dishwasher.

None of these tasks kept her thoughts occupied, and she ran her conversation with Liam over and over in her head, wishing she'd explained about Noah so Liam would understand why it was so important that she maintain a professional distance.

After half an hour she'd run out of tasks to occupy her in the kitchen and carried Maggie upstairs. The baby was almost half-asleep and showed no signs of rousing as Hadley settled her into the crib. For a long time she stared down at the motherless child, her heart aching as she contemplated how fond she'd become of the baby and realized that the end of January was fast approaching.

Soon she wouldn't have to worry over Maggie's welfare. Liam would find another nanny. It shouldn't make her heart ache, and yet it did. Hadley began to pace the comfortable guest room. Once again she'd let her heart lead instead of her head. Nor was it only her charge who had slipped beneath her skin. Liam had skirted her defenses as well. Earlier that day she'd accepted that Liam wasn't Maggie's father, but yet he'd demonstrated a willingness to step up and raise his niece, and that said a lot about his character.

Hadley stopped to peer out the window but could see nothing but fat white flakes falling past the glass. The day she'd driven up the driveway to the ranch house, she'd never dreamed that the crush she'd developed on him a decade earlier might have been lying dormant all these years. Born of hero worship and adolescent fantasies, it shouldn't have survived all the life lessons Hadley had learned. Her guilt over the role she'd played in Anna's accident, her poor judgment with Noah, the financial consequences of choosing the wrong career. All of these should have made her incapable of acting foolishly.

So far they had.

But that was before Liam Wade reentered her life. Before, she couldn't think about the man without longing to fall into bed with him, ignoring all consequences for the chance to be wildly happy for a few hours.

The baby made a sound, and Hadley went to make sure she was still asleep. Over the past week, Maggie had grown more vocal as she slept.

Hadley settled a light blanket over the baby, knowing she was fussing for no good reason. She still couldn't calm the agitation that zinged along her nerves in the aftermath of turning aside Liam's advances during dinner.

"I should have just slept with him," she murmured, the declaration sounding unbearably loud in the silent house. Then at least she'd have a good reason to regret her actions.

"It's not too late to change your mind," a low male voice said from the doorway.

Startled, Hadley whirled in Liam's direction. Heat seared her cheeks as she spotted him lounging against the door jam, an intense gleam in his half-lidded eyes. "I thought you went out."

"I did, but it wasn't any fun without you." He advanced toward her, his intent all too clear.

When his arms went around her, pulling her tight against his strong body, Hadley stopped resisting. This is what she wanted. Why fight against something that felt this right?

"Kiss me quick before I change my mind," she told him, her head falling back so she could meet his gaze. "And don't stop."

She laced her fingers through his hair as his mouth seized hers. Nerve endings writhing like live electric wires, she lost all concept of gravity. Up. Down. Left. Right. Without Liam's arms anchoring her to him, she would have shot into space like an overheated bottle rocket.

After the first hard press of his lips to hers, Liam's kiss gentled and slowed. He took his time ravishing her mouth with a bit of pressure here and a flick of his tongue there. Hadley panted in a mix of excitement and frustration. He'd been so greedy for that first kiss. She'd expected what followed would be equally fast and demanding.

"Your lips are amazing," he murmured, nipping at her lower lip. "Soft. Pliant. I could spend all night just kissing you."

Pleasure speared downward as his tongue dipped into the shallow indents left behind by his tender bite. "Other parts of me are just as interesting." She arched her back and rubbed her breasts against his chest, hoping he'd take the hint and relieve their ache.

"I imagine you will provide an unlimited source of fascination." He nuzzled his lips against her neck and bracketed her hips with his long fingers, pulling her against his erection. "Shall we go to my room and see?"

"Oh yes."

He surprised her by scooping her into his arms and carrying her next door. He set her on her feet in the middle of the dark room and pushed her to arm's length.

"I'm going to turn on the fireplace so we have some light. Then I'm going to take off your clothes and spend the rest of the night pleasuring every inch of your body."

His words left her breathless and giddy. "That sounds great," she replied, reaching out to the footboard for balance. "But I demand equal time to get to know you."

White teeth flashed in the darkness as he shot her a wolfish smile. "I love a woman who knows what she wants."

While he crossed to the enormous stone fireplace, Hadley took advantage of his back being turned to strip off her sweater and shimmy out of her black stretch pants. Clad only in a pale blue camisole and bikini briefs, she shivered in anticipation. The gas fireplace lit with a *whoosh*, and Liam turned back to her as flames began to cast flickering shadows around the room. In the dimness, his eyes seemed impossibly bright as his gaze traveled over her.

"You are gorgeous."

Although his tone gave the words a sincerity she appreciated, Hadley doubted she measured up to the women he'd been with in the past. "So are you." A sudden rush of shyness made her sound flip, but Liam didn't seem to notice.

He held out his hand. "Come here."

She couldn't have resisted his command even if her feet had been glued to the floor. More than anything she wanted his hands on her.

Together they stripped off his sweater and the long-sleeve shirt beneath. Firelight highlighted the perfection of his arms, shoulders and abs as her fingers trailed along his hot, silky skin.

"You have such an amazing body," she murmured, marveling at the perfection of every hard muscle. "I'm a little worried that you'll be disappointed in me."

He chuckled. "You have nothing to fear. You are beautiful in every way."

As if to demonstrate that, his hands began to slide upward, catching the hem of her camisole and riding it from her hips to her ribs. Hadley closed her eyes to better savor the magic of his palms gliding over her skin and threw her head back as he reached her breasts, cupping them briefly before sweeping the camisole over her head.

"I was right," he murmured, dropping to his knees to press a kiss to her abdomen.

Hadley quaked as his mouth opened and he laved her skin from belly button to hip. With his head cupped in her hands, she fought to maintain her balance as his fingers hooked in her panties and rode them down her legs. With one knee he nudged her feet apart, and she shut her eyes as his fingers trailed upward, skimming the sensitive inside of her thighs until he reached the spot where she burned.

As his fingers brushed against her pubic hair, she cried out in surprise. He'd barely touched her, and her insides were tense and primed to explode.

"You like that." He wasn't asking a question. "What about this?"

With one finger he opened her and slipped into her wetness. Hadley gasped as pleasure hammered her. Her knees began to shake, threatening to topple her.

"I can't...stand."

He cupped her butt in his hands and steadied her. "I've got you, baby. Just let go."

Her knees buckled, and Liam guided her downward and just a little forward so she ended up straddling his thighs, her breasts flattened against his hard chest. He cupped her head in his hand and brought their lips together once more. This kiss, deep and hungry, held none of the gentle restraint he'd shown earlier. It was a demonstration of his passion for her, and she was enthralled by his need.

"You need to get naked," she gasped as he rolled her beneath him on the thick, fluffy throw rug.

"Soon."

His mouth trailed moisture down her neck and over the upper curve of her breast. As delicious as it was to be slowly devoured by him, the desire clawing at her was building to a painful crescendo. She writhed beneath him, her sensitive inner thighs rasping against his soft corduroy pants as she lifted her knees to shift him deeper into the cradle of her hips.

"Oh, Liam. That's so good."

He'd taken one nipple into his mouth, and the erotic tug sharpened her longing. She ached to feel him buried inside her. Her nails bit into his sides, breath coming in shallow pants as he rocked his hips and drove his erection against her.

When she slipped her hands between them and went for the button that held his trousers closed, he caught her wrists and raised her arms over her head.

"Patience," he murmured before turning his attention to her other breast.

She thrashed her head from side to side as sensation overwhelmed her. Trapped as she was beneath him, Hadley was still able to rotate her hips and grind herself against his hard length. Liam groaned and his lips trailed down her body.

It had never been this good before. Fire consumed her at Liam's every kiss. His hot breath skated across her sensitive flesh. Suddenly her hands were free. Liam continued to slide lower; his shoulders shifted between her thighs, spreading her wide. He grazed his fingertips across her nipples, ripping a moan from her.

Before she'd even registered the pleasure of his large hands cupping her breasts, he dipped his tongue into her hot wet core and sent her spiraling into orbit. Anticipation had been gnawing on her all day, and Liam's expert loving drove her fast and hard into her first orgasm. As it ripped through her, Hadley panted his name. His fingers dug into her backside, holding her tight against his mouth as she shuddered and came in what felt like endless waves of pleasure.

"Nice," she murmured. "Very, very, very nice."

Once her body lay lifeless in the aftermath of her climax, Liam dropped a light kiss on her abdomen and left her to strip off the rest of his clothes. Despite the lack of strength in her limbs, Hadley struggled up onto her elbows to better watch his gorgeous body emerge.

She was awed by his broad shoulders, bulging biceps, washboard abs, but when he stripped off his trousers and she got a glimpse of his strong thighs and the spectacular chiseling of his firm butt, she forgot how to breathe. His erection sprang out as he peeled off his underwear, and her gaze locked on its rigid length.

She licked her lips.

"Do that again and this won't last long," Liam growled as he withdrew a condom from his wallet and made quick work of sliding it on.

She raised an eyebrow. "You're prepared?"

"I've been prepared since the day you walked into my house."

His impassioned declaration made her smile. She held out her arms to him and he lowered himself onto her. Almost immediately the tip of him found where she needed him most, but he held back and framed her face with his hands.

"I don't take this next step lightly," he told her, showing way more restraint than Hadley could manage at the moment.

As much as she appreciated what he was trying to communicate about the depth of his desire for her, she shied away from letting his affirmation into her heart. If this wasn't about two people enjoying an enormous amount of sexual chemistry, she might lose herself to the fantasy that they had a future. Where Liam was concerned, she had to maintain her head.

But all perspective was lost as he kissed her. Not waiting for him to take charge, she drove her tongue into his mouth and let him taste her passion and longing. Something in her soul clicked into place as she fisted her hands in his hair and felt him slide into her in one smooth stroke.

They moaned together and broke off the kiss to pant in agitated gasps.

"Like that," she murmured, losing herself in Liam's intense gaze. She tipped her hips and urged him deeper. "Just like that."

"There's more," he promised, beginning to move, sliding out of her with delicious deliberation before thrusting home.

"That's…" She lost the words as he found the perfect rhythm.

And then it was all heat and friction and a rapidly building pressure in her loins that demanded every bit of her attention. Being crushed beneath Liam's powerful body as he surged inside her was perhaps the most amazing experience of Hadley's life. She'd never known such delirious joy. He was passionate, yet sensitive to her body in a way no one had ever been before.

The beginnings of a second orgasm caught her in its grip. Liam continued his movements, driving her further and further toward fulfillment without taking his own. In a blurry part of her mind, she recognized that and dug her fingers into his back.

"Come with me," she urged, closer now.

"Yes."

At his growl she began to break apart. "Now."

His thrusts grew more frantic. She clung to him as wave after wave of pleasure broke over her. Liam began to shudder as he reached his own climax. She thought she heard her name on his lips as a thousand pinpoints of light exploded inside her. He was everything to her, and for a long, satisfying moment, nothing else mattered.

The weather cleared after thirty-six hours, but neither Liam nor Hadley looked forward to heading back to Texas when the airports reopened. What had happened between them was too new, its metamorphosis incomplete. Liam dreaded the return to reality. The demands of the ranch were sure to overwhelm him, and he wanted more time alone with Hadley.

The wheels of the Cessna Mustang touched down on the Royal airport runway and a sense of melancholy overwhelmed Liam. He sighed as he came in sight of his hangar. The last four days had been perfect. The solitude was exactly what he'd needed to break through Hadley's shell and reach the warm, wonderful woman beneath.

She was funny and sensual. He'd loved introducing her to new foods and wines. She'd matched his ardor in bed and demonstrated a curiosity that amused him. Once she'd let loose, she'd completely mesmerized him. He hadn't been able to get enough of her. And when they were too exhausted to move, he'd held her in his arms and enjoyed the peaceful sounds of her breathing.

He'd never felt in tune with a woman like this. Part of it was likely due to the year off he'd taken to reevaluate his priorities. Hadley was the package. She captivated him both in and out of bed and let him know pretty fast that his past practices in dealing with women weren't going to work on her. He had to be original. She deserved nothing but his best.

Maggie fussed as he locked up the plane. She hadn't slept much on the way home and was probably overtired. He watched Hadley settle the baby into the car seat and sensed the change in the air. Hadley's expression had grown serious, and her eyes lost their infectious sparkle. Playtime was over. She was back on the job.

"She's going to be fine as soon as she gets home and settled into her crib," Hadley said, coaxing the baby to take her pacifier.

"Maybe you should spend the night in case she doesn't settle down."

Hadley shook her head. "I'll stay until you get back from checking in at the ranch, but I can't stay all night."

"Not even if I need you?"

"You'll do just fine without me."

He wasn't sure if she had missed his meaning or if she was pretending not to understand that he wanted her to spend the night with him. Either way, she'd put enough determination behind her declaration to let him know no amount of persuasion was going to change her mind.

"I'm going to miss you," he said, trying a different approach.

"And I'm going to miss you," she replied, her voice brisk and not the least bit romantic. "But that was Colorado and this is Texas. We had a nice time, but it's over."

To Liam's shock, he realized he was back to square one. "I think it takes two people to decide it's over."

"You're my boss. We just need to get things back to normal."

"Or we need to change what normal is."

She didn't look happy. "I'm not sure what you mean."

"We made a great start getting to know each other these last few days. I'd like to continue."

"I don't feel comfortable in that sort of arrangement."

"Then why don't you quit?" He would not fire her. She needed to choose to be with him. "If it's about the money, I'll pay you until the end of the month."

Her mouth popped open, but before she could speak, Maggie let loose a piercing wail. "Why don't we talk about this later? I really think Maggie needs to get home."

Liam agreed, but hated the idea of postponing the conversation. He wanted to batter her with arguments until she came around to his point of view. Giving her space to think would only give her space to fortify her defenses.

"Fine. But we will talk later."

Only they didn't. By the time Liam returned from the ranch offices, it was close to midnight. Hadley was half-dead on her feet, only just having gotten Maggie to sleep after a rough evening. She was in no condition to listen to his arguments for continuing what they'd begun in Colorado, and he had to watch in frustrated silence as she put Waldo in his carrier and drove away.

With disappointment buzzing in his thoughts like a pesky fly, he expected sleep to elude him. But he'd underestimated his own weariness and shortly after his head hit the pillow, he fell asleep.

When the dream came, it didn't feature Hadley, but his mother. They stood in the ranch house's entry hall and he was desperately afraid. She was leaving. He clung to her hand and begged her not to go. She tugged hard against his grip, her face a mask of disgust.

"Mommy, don't go."

"Why would I want to stay with you? I left because I couldn't bear to be trapped in this prison of a ranch in the middle of nowhere."

"But I need you."

"I never wanted to be a mother. You and your brother were a mistake."

She ripped free and strode through the front door without ever looking back. Liam followed her, but it was as if he moved through mud. His short legs couldn't propel him fast enough, and he reached the broad wraparound porch just in time to see her taillights disappear down the driveway.

Liam woke in a sweat. His throat ached and heart pounded as he recalled his mother's words. As realistic as the exchange had felt, he recalled no such event from his childhood. His subconscious had merely been reacting to Hadley's evasiveness. So why hadn't his dream featured her?

Lingering pain carved up his chest. He felt weak and unsteady. A child's fear pummeled him. Buried deep in his mind was the horror of being rejected by his mother. She was supposed to love him and care for him. Instead, she'd demonstrated no remorse when she'd abandoned her sons to pursue her real estate career.

And it was this defining fact that had caused him to never fully invest himself in romantic relationships. He couldn't bear the idea of giving his heart to a woman only to have her choose something else over him. Deep down, what he craved was lasting love.

His heart had led him to Hadley. And given the timing of his dream, his subconscious was worried that he'd made a huge mistake.

Hadley was in the nursery folding a freshly laundered basket of Maggie's clothes when Liam appeared. He'd been subdued and circumspect around her the last couple days, and she suspected she'd done too good a job convincing him that what had happened between them in Vail had been a singular event never to be repeated.

But that wasn't at all what she wanted. She was pretty

sure she'd fallen in love with him during those four days. And that left her in a quandary.

"I know it's short notice," he said. "But will you be my date for the grand reopening of Royal Memorial's west wing tomorrow night?"

The word *date* caused a spike in Hadley's heartbeat. She told herself to stop being stupid.

"Sure. What time should I have Maggie ready?"

"Not Maggie." His green eyes pierced her facade of professionalism. "You. It's a cocktail party complete with adult beverages, finger food and fancy duds." He kept his voice light, but his expression was stony.

"Of course I'll go with you." She matched his tone, kept her glee hidden. "I've heard wonderful things about the new wing. You and the other members of the Texas Cattleman's Club were instrumental in raising the funds that enabled the restoration to move forward, weren't you?"

"We felt it was important for the community to get the hospital back to one hundred percent as soon as possible." He took her hand, threaded his fingers through hers. "How about I pick you up at seven?"

Her brain short-circuited at the way he was staring at their joined hands. As if the simple contact was at once comforting and a puzzle he couldn't figure out.

"Sure." Before she recognized what she planned to do, Hadley stepped into Liam's space and lifted onto her toes to plant a kiss on his lips.

All day long she'd been thinking about how much she wanted to be in his arms. Not to feel the stirring passion of his lovemaking, but the heart-wrenching bliss of their connection, which consisted of both sexual and spiritual components. The blend was different from anything she'd ever known, and she'd begun to neglect her defenses.

Liam brought their clasped hands to his chest and slid his free hand beneath her hair to cup her head. He explored her lips with tantalizing pressure, giving her the merest taste of passion. Although she'd initiated the kiss, she was happy to let him set the pace.

When at last his lips lifted from hers, they were both breathing unsteadily.

"I've been thinking about kissing you all day," he murmured, lips trailing over her ear, making her shudder. "I can't concentrate anymore. The entire ranch staff thinks I've lost my mind."

His words excited a flurry of goose bumps. "It's that way for me, too. I forgot to put a diaper back on Maggie before I put her back in her Onesie this morning. And then I made her bottle and put it into the cupboard instead of the container of formula."

"Will you stay at the ranch tomorrow night after the party?"

She wanted to very much, but would this interfere with her determination not to get emotionally involved? "If you wish."

"I very much wish."

"Then that's what I'll do."

Nine

Liam wasn't sure how he was going to make it through the grand opening, when all he could think about was what he had to look forward to afterward. He pulled his truck into a visitor space at Hadley's apartment building and stepped out. For tonight's event he'd exchanged denim and plaid in favor of a custom-tailored charcoal suit.

Anticipation zipped along his nerve endings as he pushed the button in the entry vestibule that would let Hadley know he'd arrived. Her voice sounded distorted as she told him to come up. Her apartment was on the second floor. He stepped into the elevator, feeling the give of the cables as it adjusted to his weight. The building had obviously seen a lot of tenants, because it showed wear and tear in the carpets, layers of paint and light fixtures.

Standing before Hadley's door, Liam paused to assess his state of agitation. Had he ever been nervous going to pick up a woman for a date? Yet here he stood, palms sweating, heart thundering, mouth dry.

The door opened before he lifted his hand to knock. Hadley looked surprised to see him standing in the hallway. Waldo rushed forward to wind himself around Liam's legs.

"Hi." She gestured him in. "I thought maybe the elevator had decided to be fussy again."

He picked up the cat without taking his eyes from Hadley and stepped into her apartment. "You look beautiful."

She wore a figure-skimming sleeveless black dress with a round neckline and a half-circle cutout that bared her cleavage. Despite there being nothing overtly provocative about the style, Liam thought she looked incredibly sexy. She'd pinned her blond waves up in a complicated hairstyle that looked as if it could tumble onto her shoulders at any second. And he badly wanted to make that happen. Body alive with cravings better reserved for later that evening, he shifted his gaze to her only jewelry, a pair of long crystal earrings that swung in sassy rhythm as she tipped her head and regarded him curiously.

"Thank you." Her half smile captivated him. "You look nice, as well. I'll grab my purse and we can get going." She picked up a small black clutch and a sheer red scarf sparkling with clusters of sequins that she draped over her shoulders. It added a flamboyant touch to her otherwise monochrome black ensemble.

Realizing he was staring at her like a smitten teenager, Liam cleared his throat. His brain was having trouble summoning words. "All set?"

"Are you expecting a large crowd tonight?" she asked as she fit her key into the lock and set the dead bolt.

"About a hundred. Those responsible for coordinating the fund-raising efforts and the largest contributors."

"What a wonderful thing you've done."

Her glowing praise lightened his step. He laced his fingers through hers and lifted her hand to brush a kiss across her knuckles. "It was a group effort," he said, feeling unusually humble. "But thank you."

In truth, he was proud of the work he and the other members of the Texas Cattleman's Club had done in the aftermath of the tornado. As leaders in the community, they'd banded together during the time of crisis and although progress had been slow, they'd restored the town to its former state.

The drive from Hadley's apartment to the hospital took ten minutes. Liam filled the time with a description about an outfit his cousin Ivy had bought for Maggie that featured a chambray Onesie with three tiers of ruffles and a crocheted cowboy hat and boots.

"Complete with yarn spurs." Liam shook his head in mock dismay.

"How adorable." Hadley regarded his expression with a wry smile. "You are just going to have to get used to the fact that girls love to dress up and look pretty."

"I know," he grumbled, knowing she loved to scold him. "But is it really going to be all frilly stuff and hair bows?"

"Yes."

Liam pulled to a stop in front of the hospital's new west wing entrance, and the look he gave Hadley made her laugh. A year ago he never would have imagined himself discussing an infant's wardrobe, much less with a beautiful woman.

A valet opened the passenger door and helped Hadley out of the truck. Liam was grinning as he accepted the ticket from the uniformed attendant and caught up with Hadley, sliding his hand over her hip in a not-so-subtle show of ownership. She sent him an unguarded smile of such delight, his chest hurt. If this was heartache, bring it on.

"This is amazing," Hadley murmured as they entered the spacious lobby of the redesigned west wing, taking in the patterned marble floors and triangular glass ceiling over the entrance. In the center of the room, a bronze statue of a cowboy roping a running cow had the names of all those who'd lost their lives during the tornado etched around the base. "A wonderful tribute."

Spying Case Baxter, Liam drew Hadley toward the rancher, who had eyes only for the redhead beside him.

"Case," Liam called to gain his attention.

The president of the Cattleman's Club looked away from his fiancée and blinked as if to reorient himself. At last his gaze focused on Liam.

"Hey, Liam." His teeth flashed as he extended his hand to meet Liam's. "Mellie, you've met Liam Wade."

"Of course." A friendly smile curved her lips. Her green eyes darted toward Hadley before settling back on Liam. "At the reception when Case was elected president."

"And this is Hadley Stratton." Liam didn't explain how they knew each other. Why introduce her as Maggie's nanny when she'd become so much more? "Mellie Winslow and Case Baxter, our club president."

The two couples finished exchanging greetings and Case spoke. "Gotta hand it to you, Liam." He gestured around, his grin wide, posture relaxed. "This is one hell of a facility."

"Have you toured the neonatal unit?" Mellie asked.

"We just arrived," Hadley admitted, completely at ease tucked into the half circle of Liam's left arm. After their conversation in Vail, he'd half expected her to balk at going public with their developing relationship.

"The whole wing is really terrific," Mellie was saying, "but that unit in particular is very impressive."

Liam agreed. He'd seen the neonatal facility during his many trips to the hospital in his role as chairman of the fund-raising committee, but he was looking forward to showing it to Hadley.

"Why don't we head up now," he suggested, seeing Hadley's interest. There would be plenty of time later to catch up with Mac, Jeff Hartley and other members of the Texas Cattleman's Club. "We'll catch up with you later," he told Case.

"They seem like a nice couple," Hadley commented as they waited for the elevator that would take them to the maternity ward on the fourth floor.

"I don't know Mellie all that well, but Case is a great guy and they appear happy."

The elevator doors opened, and Liam gestured Hadley ahead of him.

Despite the crowd gathered to party in the lobby, they had the elevator to themselves. As soon as the car began to move, Liam tugged Hadley into his arms and dropped his lips to hers.

The instant Liam kissed her, Hadley wrapped her arms around his neck and yielded to his demand. Frantic to enjoy the few seconds of isolation, they feasted on each other. But all too soon, a *ding* announced that they'd reached their floor, cutting short their impassioned embrace.

"Damn these modern elevators," Liam muttered, his hands sliding off her body.

Hadley, her cheeks hot in the aftermath of the kiss, smiled foolishly. She surveyed his chiseled lips, searching for any sign that her red lipstick had rubbed off. Taking the hand Liam offered her, she stepped past a tour group that was waiting to head downstairs.

"Let's see if we can catch that tour," he said, tugging her down the hallway toward a group of well-dressed guests listening to a tall, handsome man in his late thirties.

"Next is our neonatal unit," the man said, gesturing down the hall as he started forward.

"That's Dr. Parker Reese," Liam explained, tucking Hadley's hand into the crook of his arm. "He's a neonatal specialist. Brilliant guy. We're lucky to have him."

It was hard to focus on Dr. Reese's description of the neonatal unit's state-of-the-art equipment and dedicated staff while her senses were filled with the scent, sight and feel of Liam so close beside her.

He stiffened, dragging Hadley out of her musings. She returned her attention to the speaker only to discover Dr.

Reese had passed off the tour to a slender nurse with blond hair pulled back into a bun and a brisk way of speaking.

"We call her Janey Doe," the nurse said, a hint of sadness clouding her direct green gaze. "She is holding her own, but each day is a struggle. However, thanks to Dr. Reese…" The nurse glanced up at the tall doctor, and Hadley got the impression that equal parts personal and professional admiration curved her lips.

The crowd began to follow Dr. Reese toward the birthing suites, but Liam showed no interest in continuing on. He made a beeline straight for the nurse and introduced himself.

"Hello, I'm Liam Ward. And this is Hadley Stratton."

"Clare Connelly." The nurse shook their hands. "Thank you for all your hard work on the restoration of this wing. It's such an amazing facility to work in."

"It was an important project for our town." Although his words were courteous, his tone was strained. "I was wondering if you could tell me a little bit more about Janey Doe."

Knowing that she had missed a big chunk of the story, Hadley scanned Liam's expression, noticed his tight lips, the muscle jumping in his jaw and wondered at his interest.

"She was found on the floor of a truck stop thirty miles from here…"

"No sign of her mother?" Liam's question reverberated with disgust.

Clare shook her head slowly. "None, I'm afraid."

"You mean she just left her there?" Hadley's chest tightened. "How could she do something like that?"

"She was probably young and scared. Janey was very small and obviously premature. It's possible the mother thought she was dead and freaked out."

Hadley appreciated how Clare stuck up for Baby Janey's mother but could see that none of her assumptions had eased Liam's displeasure. He was staring into the neonatal unit, his attention laser focused on the middle incubator. Was Maggie on his mind? Without knowing for certain that Maggie was related to Liam, Diane Garner had left her granddaughter in his care. Or was he thinking how his own mother had left him to be raised by his grandfather?

"What will happen to her?" Hadley asked, her own gaze drawn toward the incubator and the precious bundle. The baby was hooked up to a feeding tube, oxygen and monitors, making it impossible to get a clear look at her face.

"She'll go into foster care and eventually be adopted." Although the words were hopeful, the nurse's smile was strained.

Hadley recognized that look. She'd seen it on the faces of plenty of her fellow nannies who'd grown too attached to their charges.

"Thank you for your time." Liam glanced down at Hadley, his expression unreadable. "Shall we rejoin the party?"

All warmth had been leeched from his manner by the story of Baby Janey. Hadley nodded and strolled back toward the elevator at Liam's side. Although her hand remained tucked in his arm, the emotional distance between them was as wide as an ocean. She recognized that this had nothing to do with her. Liam had retreated behind walls she couldn't penetrate, defenses a young boy had erected to deal with his mother's abandonment.

"Why don't we get out of here," Hadley suggested as they descended in the elevator. "I don't think you're in the mood for a party anymore."

"You're right." One side of his lips kicked up. His gaze warmed as he bent down to brush a kiss across her lips. "But I should at least spend an hour here. If for no other reason than to show off my gorgeous date."

Hadley blushed at the compliment. It didn't matter what

anyone else thought of her looks; as long as she could bask in Liam's sizzling admiration, she felt flawless.

By the time the elevator doors opened, Liam seemed to have gotten past whatever had affected him in the neonatal unit. Once again the charming rascal she adored, he worked his way around the room, collecting smiles and promises of funds for several pieces of equipment the hospital still needed.

Watching him work, Hadley reveled in his charisma and marveled at his ability to strike just the right chord with everyone he met. This is what made him an astute businessman and a masterful horseman. He didn't approach every situation with the same tactic.

"I'm ready to get out of here if you are," he murmured in her ear an hour later.

"Absolutely," she replied, anticipating what awaited them back at the ranch house.

On the ride home, Liam lapsed back into silence, his public persona put aside once more. Hadley stared at his profile in concern. Her hopes for a romantic evening fled. Liam's troubled thoughts preoccupied him.

As Liam unlocked the front door, Hadley set aside her disappointment and decided to see if she could get him to open up. "How about I make some coffee and we talk about what's bothering you?"

Liam's chin dipped in ascent. "I'll get a fire started in the den."

Once she got the coffee brewing, Hadley ran upstairs to check on Maggie. She found the baby sleeping and Candace in the rocking chair, reading on her tablet. The housekeeper looked up in surprise as Hadley crossed to the crib.

"You're home early. Did you have fun?"

"It was a nice party. The facilities are wonderful." Hadley knew she hadn't directly answered Candace's question. While she'd enjoyed the company and the conversation,

Liam's mood after learning about Janey Doe had unsettled her. "Thanks for watching Maggie. Any problems?"

Candace got to her feet. "She went to sleep at eight and hasn't made a peep since."

"Good." Maggie's hair was soft beneath Hadley's fingers as she brushed a strand off the baby's forehead. "I made some coffee if you're interested in joining us for a cup."

"No, thanks. I'm almost done with this book. I'm going to head back to the carriage house and finish it."

The two women headed downstairs. Liam was in the kitchen and gave Candace a cheerful thank-you as she left. By the time the housekeeper pulled the back door shut behind her, icy air filled the space. Hadley shivered and filled the mugs Liam had fetched from the cupboard. Cradling the warm ceramic in her hands, she led the way into the den and settled on the sofa.

Liam set his mug on the mantel and chose to stand, staring into the fire. "I'm sorry I was such bad company tonight."

"You weren't bad company." Hadley was careful not to let her disappointment show. "Obviously something is bothering you. Do you feel like talking about it?"

"It was hearing about Janey Doe."

"That was a very upsetting story." She refrained from adding her own opinion on the subject, wanting Liam to share his thoughts.

"Her mother just leaving her like that. On the floor of a public bathroom. She could have died."

Hadley kept her voice neutral. "She was fortunate that someone found her."

"I thought it was bad that Maggie's grandmother left her with us. This is so much worse. How could any mother abandon her child like that?"

"Not every woman is cut out for motherhood." Hadley

thought about all the families she'd worked for in the last five years and all the stories shared by her fellow nannies. "Sometimes the responsibility is more than they can handle."

"You mean they wish they'd never given birth."

Trying her best to hide a wince, Hadley responded, "I mean that parenting can be challenging, and sometimes if a woman has to do it alone, she might not feel capable."

"Perhaps if she's young and without financial means, I could understand, but what can you say about a woman who has family and fortune and turns her back on her children so she can pursue her career?"

Not wanting to sound as if she were picking sides, Hadley chose her next words carefully. "That she acted in her best interest and not in the best interest of her children."

Liam crossed to the sofa and joined Hadley. A huge gust of air escaped his lungs as he picked up her hand and squeezed her fingers. "Maggie must never know that her grandmother left her with us the way she did. I won't have her wondering why she didn't want to keep her."

This was the true source of Liam's disquiet, Hadley realized. Whether he acknowledged it or not, being abandoned by his mother had sabotaged his ability to trust women. And where did that leave Hadley?

Liam could feel the concern rolling off Hadley as he spoke. He'd grown attuned to her moods since their days in Vail and didn't have to see her expression to know her thoughts.

Hadley covered their clasped hands with her free one and squeezed. "It's okay to be angry with your mother for not being there for you."

The knot of emotions in his chest tightened at her words. Not once as a child had he seen his grandfather demonstrate anything but understanding toward the daughter who'd run out on her children. Liam had grown up thinking that what his mother had done was acceptable, while inside him was a howling banshee of anger and hurt that was never given a voice.

"You might feel better if you talked through how it made you feel."

"I don't know how to begin." The words, long bottled up inside him, were poised to explode. "I grew up thinking it was okay that she chose to leave us with Grandfather."

"Why?"

"She had a career that she loved, and like you said earlier, she really wasn't cut out to be a mom. She got pregnant when she was seventeen. Our father was on the rodeo circuit and had no interest in settling down to raise a family. Mother felt the same way. Grandfather always said she had big dreams." Liam offered up a bitter laugh. "I guess Kyle and I are lucky she decided to have us at all."

Hadley's shocked intake of breath left Liam regretting the venomous statement.

"You don't mean that."

"No," he agreed. "Although I've thought it a hundred times, I don't think she ever considered terminating her pregnancy. In that respect, she didn't take the easy way out."

"Getting back to what you said earlier, growing up did you really think that it was okay she left you with your grandfather, or was that just a coping mechanism?"

"In my mind, I understood her decision. I can't explain to you why that made sense. Maybe because it happened when we were babies and I never knew any different. But recently I started realizing that deep down inside, I hated her for leaving us."

He'd coped by becoming a champion rider. Throwing himself into competition had preoccupied him in his teenage years. The closer he'd gotten to manhood, the less he thought about his mother's absence. The day he'd kissed a girl for the first time, he'd stopped caring.

"Grandfather wasn't exactly the most affectionate guy in the world, but he loved us in his tough-guy way. It might have been different if we were girls, but growing up on the ranch, we had more father figures than anyone could ever want."

"You sound very well adjusted." Her tone said otherwise. "Do you think not having a mother affected your relationships with women?"

"You mean because I never got married?"

"You have a well-earned reputation for being a playboy. I can't imagine you trusted your heart after what your mother did."

"I'll admit to having a wandering eye when it came to women, but that's changed."

"Just because you think you're ready to settle down doesn't mean you've learned to trust." She smiled to take the sting out of the words, but her eyes reflected wariness.

"You're the first woman I've been with in a year," he reminded her, voice rasping as frustration overcame him. "I think that proves I'm already settled down. And I trust you."

Doubt continued to shadow her eyes. He shifted on the couch, angling his body toward her. Gripped by the urgent need to kiss her, Liam dipped his head, shortening the distance between them. He would demonstrate that he was serious about her.

Before he could kiss her, Hadley set her fingertips on his lips. "Thank you for sharing how you felt about your mother not being around. I know that couldn't have been easy."

"It wasn't." And yet it had been a relief to share his anger and sense of betrayal with her. "Thank you for listening."

A moment earlier he'd had something to prove, but the mood was no longer right for seduction. Instead, he planted a friendly kiss on her cheek and held her in a tight hug.

"Let's go upstairs," she murmured, her hands sliding beneath his suit coat, fingers splaying over his back. "I want to make love to you."

At her declaration Liam took a massive hit to his solar plexus. Pulse quickening, he caught her by the hand and drew her toward the stairs. They climbed together in a breathless rush. By the time they reached his bedroom, he was light-headed and more than a little frantic to get them both naked.

Once they crossed the threshold, Hadley plucked the pins from her hair, and it tumbled around her shoulders. Liam came to stand behind her, pushing the thick mass of blond hair away from her neck so he could kiss the slender column and make her shiver. He stripped off his jacket and shirt before turning his attention to the zipper of her dress. With more urgency than finesse, he stroked the dress down her body. When it pooled at her feet, he skimmed his palms back upward, hesitating over the ticklish spot beside her hip bones and investigating each bump of her ribs. The rise and fall of her chest grew less rhythmic as he unfastened her strapless bra and tossed the scrap of fabric on to a nearby chair.

Her hand came up to the back of his head as he cupped her breasts in his palms, thumbs flicking over her tight nipples. She shuddered, her head falling back against his chest, eyes closed as she surrendered to his touch. Although the tightness in his groin demanded that he stop all the foreplay and get down to business, Liam had no intention of rushing. He'd rather savor the silken heat of her skin and bring her body as much pleasure as it could take before seeking his own release.

She turned in his arms, her soft breasts flattening

against his chest as she lifted on tiptoe and sought his mouth with hers. She cupped his face in her hands to hold him still while her tongue darted forward to toy with his. Liam crushed her to him, his fingers dipping below her black lace panties to swallow one butt cheek and lift her against his erection.

They both groaned as he rocked against her. She lifted her foot and wrapped her leg around his hips, angling the bulge behind his zipper into the warm, wet cleft between her thighs. The move unraveled all of Liam's good intentions. He plucked her off her feet and moved toward the bed. She set the soles of her feet against his calves to keep him anchored between her thighs and impatiently removed his belt. It was torture to let her undress him. Every time her fingers glanced off his erection, he ground his teeth and bit back a groan. Only by watching the play of emotions race across her beautiful features was he able to maintain his control. By the time she'd slid open his zipper and pushed the pants down his thighs, his nerves screamed with impatience.

Liam stripped off pants, shoes, socks and underwear without ever taking his eyes off Hadley. With a sensual smile she moved backward, making room for him on the mattress. He stalked onto the bed, fitting between her spread thighs, covering her torso with his before claiming her lips in a hard kiss and her body with a single deep thrust.

He loved the way her hips lifted to meet his. How she arched her back and took him all the way in. Her chest vibrated with a moan. A matching sound gathered in his lungs. For a long moment they lay without moving, lips and tongues engaged.

Framing her face in his hands, Liam lifted his lips from hers and stared into her eyes. "Thank you for being my date tonight." It wasn't what he'd intended to say, but nevertheless his words pleased her.

"Thank you for asking. I had a lovely time."

"Lovely?" He grinned. "Let's see if we can't upgrade that to fantastic."

Her eyebrows lifted, daring him to try, while her fingers stroked down his sides. "We're off to a wonderful start."

Liam nuzzled his face into her throat and began to move inside her. "We certainly are."

Ten

The night after the party at the hospital, Hadley was back on the neonatal floor she and Liam had toured. After receiving Maggie's blood work back, Dr. Stringer had determined she should undergo phototherapy treatments for her jaundice. Despite being overwhelmed with ranch business, Liam had accompanied them, wearing his concern openly, but once he discerned how straightforward the process was, he'd relaxed.

Maggie had been stripped down to her diaper and placed in an incubator equipped with a light box that directed blue fluorescent light onto her skin. The light was meant to change the bilirubin into a form that Maggie could more easily expel through her urine. While the procedure was simple, it also took time to work. Maggie would be in the hospital for a couple days while undergoing the treatment. Hadley had agreed to stay with her to let Liam focus on the ranch.

Hadley caught herself humming as she fed Maggie her late-afternoon bottle. After the party at the hospital and the night spent in Liam's arms, she'd stopped resisting what her heart wanted and let herself enjoy every moment of her time with Liam. Why fight against the inevitable? She'd fallen deeply in love with the man.

While a part of her couldn't help but compare what was between her and Liam to what she'd had with Noah, deep down, Hadley recognized the vast difference between the two relationships. With Noah she'd never enjoyed any sort of emotional security. As much as he'd gone on and on about how much he wanted her, how his kids adored her, she always got the sense that he was looking over her shoulder for someone else. It turned out that someone else had been his ex-wife.

Liam never once let her think she was second best. His focus was always completely on her, and Hadley found that both comforting and wildly exciting. For the first time in a long time, she'd stopped focusing on the future and lived quite happily in the moment. School would start when it started. Her time with Maggie would grow shorter. Already arrangements had been made for the new nanny to start at the end of the month. This freed Hadley from her professional responsibilities, and she was eager to see where her relationship with Liam led.

Maggie's eyelids started to droop before the bottle was finished. Hadley set it aside, lifted the infant onto her shoulder and patted her back to encourage a burp. A nurse stood by to test Maggie's bilirubin levels. The staff members were monitoring her every hour or so. Hadley was calling Liam with the results.

His concern for Maggie's welfare had warmed her when she thought the baby was his daughter. Now that she knew Maggie was his brother's child, Liam's commitment was just another reason Hadley found him so attractive.

She was tired of restraining her emotions. Liam made her happy, and she thought he felt the same way about her. When Maggie left the hospital, Hadley promised herself she would stop holding back.

Several days after the hospital party, Liam had an appointment with former Samson Oil lawyer Nolan Dane, who'd joined his father's family law practice. Recently,

Nolan had been accepted for membership in the Texas Cattleman's Club, and the more Liam got to know the man, the more he liked him. The idea that had begun percolating in his mind took on a whole new urgency on the trip back from Colorado. With Maggie in the hospital and Hadley staying with her, the notion had solidified into a plan that required a savvy lawyer.

Liam stepped into Nolan's office. "Looks like you're all settled in."

Nolan grinned. "It's taken longer than I figured on. I didn't expect to be so busy this early in my start-up."

"That must mean you're good. Looks like I've come to the right place."

"Can I offer you coffee or water before we get started?" Nolan gestured Liam into a chair at the round conference table.

"Thanks, but I'm good." While Nolan took a seat, Liam pulled out the paternity test as well as Maggie's birth certificate and her mother's death certificate that Diane Garner had sent at his request.

Nolan found a blank page on his yellow legal pad and met Liam's gaze. "What can I help you with?"

"I have a situation with my twin brother's baby." Liam explained how Maggie had come to Wade Ranch and showed Nolan the DNA results. "Maggie is definitely Kyle's daughter. As soon as I received the test back, I left messages for him on his cell and with the navy."

"How long ago was this?"

"About two weeks."

"And you haven't heard back?"

"Only that the message was delivered. He's a SEAL, which probably means he's on a mission overseas." Liam leaned forward. "And that's where my concerns lie. I don't know a lot about Kyle's domestic situation, but based on his past track record, I'm guessing he's not in a long-term relationship and certainly isn't in a position to take care of a baby."

"You're not in regular contact?"

"Not since he left Royal and joined the navy." Liam wasn't proud of the way he and Kyle had drifted apart, but growing up they'd been uniquely dissimilar in temperament and interests for identical twins.

"And it sounds like the child's grandmother, Diane Garner, is reluctant to be responsible for Maggie."

"She has serious medical issues that prevent her from taking care of Maggie. Which leaves Kyle." Liam paused to give his next words weight. "Or me."

"You want custody?"

While Liam's first instinct was to say yes, he intended to do what was best for Maggie. "I'd like to evaluate all the options."

One corner of Nolan's lips twitched. "You don't have to be diplomatic with me, Liam. I'm here to help you out. Now, what do you want?"

"I'd like custody, but what is most important is to do right by Maggie." Liam gathered his thoughts for a long moment. "I have concerns that while Kyle is off on missions, he'll have to rely on others to take care of her for extended periods of time. And what happens if he's hurt…" Or killed. But Liam couldn't go there. Most days he didn't give Kyle a thought, but sometimes a news report would catch his attention and Liam would wonder what his brother was up to.

"Do you know if Kyle and Margaret were in touch before she drove to Wade Ranch?" Nolan continued to jot down items on his legal pad. "I'm trying to get a sense of their relationship."

"I don't know, but I have to think if Kyle had any idea he was going to be a father that he would have let me know." Liam wanted to believe his brother would step up and do the right thing by his daughter. Yet the fact that Kyle hadn't been in contact disturbed Liam. "That leads me to believe that he didn't know. Either because she hadn't told him or she had the same trouble getting a hold of him I'm having."

Liam didn't add that it was possible Margaret had been nothing more than a weeklong fling for Kyle and he'd had no intention of keeping in touch.

"Because Margaret died in childbirth and she and Kyle weren't married, only her name appears on Maggie's birth certificate. Normally what would happen in this sort of case is that both parties would fill out an AOP. That's an Acknowledgment of Paternity. This form would normally be filled out and signed at the hospital. Or through a certified entity that would then file it with the Vital Statistics Unit. Unfortunately, without Margaret alive to concede that your brother is the child's father, this case will have to go to court. Of course, DNA evidence will prove Kyle's the father. But with you two being identical twins and no way of proving which one of you is the father..." After a long silence, broken only by the scratch of his pen across the legal pad, Nolan glanced up. His eyes gleamed. "I can see why you came to me. This situation is by no means clear-cut."

"No, it's not." But at least Liam had a clearer picture of what he wanted. Tension he didn't realize he'd been holding unwound from his shoulder muscles. "How do you suggest we proceed?"

"Let's find out what we can about Margaret and her time with Kyle in San Antonio. I have an investigator I've worked with there. If you give me the go-ahead, I'll contact him."

"Do you think I have a case for retaining custody of Maggie?" Before he let Kyle take Maggie away, Liam intended to make sure his brother was willing to fight for her. And fight hard.

"A lot will depend on how determined your brother is

to be a father. You and your brother aren't in contact. We should probably check on Kyle's current financial status and personal life as well and see what sort of environment Maggie would be going into. I think you're right that between the two situations, Wade Ranch promises the most stability for a baby. But a judge might reason that you're both single men and that Maggie should be with her father."

Her *single* father who might be activated at a moment's notice and be out of the country who knew how long.

"What if I were engaged?" Liam suggested, voicing what had been running through his head since his trip to Colorado. "Or married?"

Nolan nodded. "Might sway a judge. Are you?"

"Not yet." For a year Liam had pondered the benefits of settling down. All he'd been waiting for was the right woman. Hadley fit the bill in every way. She was smart, beautiful and great with Maggie. After Colorado he'd decided he'd be a complete idiot not to lock her down as soon as possible before she finished school and headed off to pursue a career elsewhere. "But I plan to pop the question to a special lady in the very near future."

Hadley rocked a sleepy Maggie as she checked out the photos of Liam's family on the walls of the ranch office.

"Thanks for bringing lunch," Liam said. "The day has been crazy."

With calving time a couple weeks away and a whole host of unexpected issues popping up, Liam and Ivy had decided to work through lunch. The weather had turned warmer and Hadley was feeling restless, so she'd offered to bring their meal to the barn.

As if Liam's words had the power to summon trouble, one of the hands appeared in the doorway. "Dean told me to stop by and see if you had an hour or so free. Sam is out sick," the hand said. "Barry is off visiting his kid in Tulsa. We could use some help cutting the cows who aren't pregnant."

"Sure." Liam shifted his weight in the direction of the door, but glanced at Hadley before taking a step. "Ever cut cattle?"

She shook her head, sensing what was coming and wondering why Liam, knowing what he did, would ask her to ride with him.

"Like to try?"

Hadley was surprised by her strong desire to say yes. "What about Maggie?"

"I'd be happy to watch her until you get back," Ivy offered, cooing at the infant. "You'd like to hang out with Cousin Ivy until they get back, wouldn't you?" Maggie waved her arms as if in agreement. "Or I can drive her back to the house if it gets too late."

"See?" Liam's eyes held a hard glint of challenge. "All settled. Let's go find you a mount."

While her gut clenched in happy anticipation of getting on a horse again, Hadley rationalized her agreement by telling herself it was work, not pleasure. She was doing something her employer requested. Never mind that he'd been trying to figure out a way to get her back in the saddle since she'd stepped into his home two and a half weeks ago.

Excitement built as he led her outside to the paddocks where they turned out the horses during the day. Twelve horses occupied four enclosures.

Liam nodded toward a palomino mare in the farthest right paddock. The only horse in the fenced-in area, she stood in the middle, tearing at the winter grass with strong white teeth. "Daisy could use some exercise. I don't think she's been ridden much in the last year. I'll get one of the guys to saddle her for you."

"I can saddle my own horse," Hadley retorted, insulted. "Besides, I'd like to get to know her a little before I get on."

"Okay. She's a nice mare. You shouldn't have any trouble with her on the ground."

As Liam's last three words registered, she glanced over at him, but discovered nothing in his expression to arouse her suspicions. Surely he wouldn't put her on a green horse after such a long absence from the saddle. Once upon a time her skills might have been first-rate, but a decade had passed since she'd used those particular muscles. Riding a horse wasn't the same as riding a bike.

"You said she hasn't been ridden much in the last year?" Hadley decided a little clarification might be in order. "But she has been ridden, right?"

"Oh, sure." Liam walked over to the fence and picked up the halter and lead rope hung on the gate. "We were going to breed her last year, but that didn't work out. So she's just been hanging around, waiting to become a mother." He opened the gate and handed Hadley the halter. "She's easy to catch. I'll meet you in that barn over there." He indicated the building that housed the horses in training. "You might want to do a couple circles in the indoor ring before we head out."

Sensing something was up despite Liam's neutral expression and bland tone, Hadley slipped the halter onto the mare and led her to the building Liam had indicated. He hadn't yet arrived, so Hadley got busy with currycomb and brush. She smiled as the mare leaned into the grooming. Obviously Daisy appreciated Hadley's efforts.

She would have preferred to take more time with the mare, but Liam showed up, leading a gorgeous bay stallion that was already saddled and ready to go. Hadley returned his nod before tossing the saddle onto Daisy's back, settling it in just the right spot and tightening the cinch as if she'd done it last week instead of ten years earlier. Working just as efficiently, she slipped the bit into the mare's mouth and fitted the headstall into place.

"Ready?"

All at once she became aware of Liam's attention and grew self-conscious. "I think so."

"Come on. I'll work the kinks out of Buzzard while you try out Daisy."

Leading Daisy, Hadley followed Liam and the bay into the arena. What if she made a complete hash of it and ended up getting dumped? While Hadley fussed with Daisy's girth and grappled with her nerves, Liam swung up onto the stallion's back. Buzzard took several steps sideways as Liam settled his weight, but quickly relaxed beneath the pressure of his rider's legs and the steadiness of Liam's hands on the reins.

The guy was an amazing rider, and Hadley felt a fangirl moment coming on. Embarrassed at her gawking, she set her foot in the stirrup. Daisy was a little shorter than Lolita, but she felt her muscles protest as she threw her leg up and over the mare's back. Before she'd completely found her balance, Daisy's muscles bunched beneath her and the mare crow-hopped a half dozen times while Hadley clung to the saddle horn, laughter puffing out of her with each jolt of Daisy's four hoofs hitting the ground.

At last the mare got her silliness out of her system and stood still while Hadley retrieved her breath.

"You okay?"

"Fine." Hadley could feel the broad smile on her face. "Is she going to be like this the whole time?"

"No. She just wanted to make sure you were going to stay on. You passed."

"She was testing me?" The notion struck Hadley as ludicrous. What sort of horse had Liam put her on?

"She's a smart horse." His lips kicked up. "Needs a smart rider."

Apparently Daisy wasn't the only one doing the testing. Hadley keyed the mare into a walk and then took five minutes to work through all her gaits. Whoever had trained the palomino had done a fabulous job. She was a dream to ride.

"Let's go cut some cattle," Hadley said, all too aware how closely Liam had been observing her.

Liam didn't think a woman's pleasure had ever been as important to him as Hadley's. Between their lovemaking in Vail and the joy she'd demonstrated cutting cattle today, especially when Daisy had kept a heifer from returning to the herd, he was convinced he would know true happiness only if he continued delighting Hadley.

Would he have felt the same a year ago? Remaining celibate for twelve months had given him a greater appreciation of companionship. Being with Hadley had enabled him to understand the difference between what he'd had with his former girlfriends and true intimacy. Granted, he'd only barely scratched the surface with her. Instinct told him she was rich with complex layers she didn't yet trust him to see. Moving past her defenses wasn't anything he wanted to rush. Or force.

He had a good thing going. Why make a mistake and risk losing her?

"That was amazing," Hadley crowed. Cheeks flushed, eyes dancing with excitement, she was as vibrant as he'd ever seen her. "You knew I'd love this when you suggested I ride her."

"She's a natural, boss," one of the ranch hands commented, his gaze lingering on Hadley longer than Liam liked.

"I figured she would be."

The urge to growl at the cowboy was nearly impossible to repress. Obviously, Liam wasn't the only one dazzled by the attractive Ms. Hadley Stratton. And since he hadn't yet staked a public claim, the rest of the male population assumed she was fair game. That situation was not to his liking. Time he did something to change it.

Liam nudged his stallion forward and cut Hadley off from the admiring cowboys with the ease of someone accustomed to working cattle. "It's late. We should be getting back to Maggie."

Her eyes lost none of their sparkle as she nodded. "I've probably strained enough muscles for one day." She laughed. "I can tell I'm going to be in pain tomorrow, but it was worth it."

"I'm glad you like Daisy." Liam decided to push his luck. "She could probably stand a little work if you felt inclined."

Hadley hesitated but shook her head. He was making progress since the last time he'd tried to persuade her to ride. He wanted her to talk to him, to share how she was feeling. They'd discussed her friend's accident, and Hadley had mulled his suggestion that she move past the guilt that she'd carried for years. Had something about that changed?

"I'm due to go back to school in a week. I don't know how I'd make time."

He'd found a permanent nanny for Maggie. Liam and Hadley had agreed that being together would not work if she was still his employee. But he was realizing that she would no longer be an everyday fixture in his life, and that was a situation he needed to fix.

"I don't mind sharing you with the horses," he said, keeping his voice casual. He'd never had to work so hard to keep from spooking a woman.

"Oh, you don't?" She gave him a wry smile. "What if I don't have enough time for either of you?"

Liam's grip on the reins tightened and Buzzard began trotting in place. If he thought she was flirting, he'd have shot back a provocative retort, but Liam had gotten to know Hadley well enough in the last few weeks to know she had serious concerns.

"Move in with me."

The offer was sudden, but he didn't surprise himself when he made it.

"You already have a full-time nanny moving in."

"Not as a nanny."

Her eyes widened. "Then as what?"

"The woman I'm crazy about." He'd never been in love and had no idea if that's what he felt for Hadley. But he'd been doing a lot of soul-searching these last few days.

"You're crazy about me?" The doubt in her voice wasn't unexpected.

He'd known she wouldn't accept his declaration without some vigorous convincing. Hadley wasn't one to forgive herself easily for past mistakes. She'd fallen for her first employer, only to have her heart torn up when the jerk got back together with his ex-wife. That wasn't a judgment error she would make a second time. And she was already skeptical of Liam's past romantic history.

"If we weren't on these damned horses I'd demonstrate just how crazy."

Liam ground his teeth at her surprise. What kept her from accepting how strong his feelings had become? The mildest of her saucy smiles provoked a befuddling rush of lust. He pondered what her opinion would be on a dozen decisions before lunch. Waking up alone in his big bed had become the most painful part of his day.

"This is happening too fast."

"I'm not going to bail on you."

"I know."

"You don't sound convinced." He was determined to change her mind. "What can I say to reassure you?"

"You don't need to say anything."

After regarding her for a long moment, he shook his head. "I've dated a lot of women."

"This is your way of convincing me to take a chance on you?"

He ignored her interruption. "Enough to recognize that how I feel about you is completely foreign to me." He saw he'd hit the wrong note with the word *foreign*. "And terrific. Scary. Fascinating. I've never been so twisted up by a woman before."

"And somehow you think this is a good thing?"

"You make me better. I feel more alive when I'm with you. Like anything is possible."

She blinked several times. "I think that's the most amazing thing anyone has ever said to me."

"I don't believe that. I do, however, believe that it might be one of the first times you've let yourself hear and trust one of my compliments." He was making progress if she'd stopped perceiving everything he said as a ploy.

"You might be right."

They'd drawn within sight of the ranch buildings, and Liam regretted how fast the ride had gone. He hadn't received an answer from Hadley, and the time to pursue the matter was fast coming to an end.

"I hope that means you're beginning to believe me when I tell you how important you've become to me."

"It's starting to sink in." She watched him from beneath her eyelashes. "But are you ready to have me move in?"

"Absolutely." His conviction rang in his answer. "But it's not the only thing I want."

This was something else he'd thought long and hard about. It wasn't just his feelings for Hadley that were driving him, but also his need to give Maggie a loving home and create for her the sort of stable family denied him and Kyle.

"No?"

"What I really want is for us to get married."

Eleven

While Hadley wondered if she'd heard him correctly, Liam pulled a ring box out of his coat pocket and extended it her way. She stared at it, her heart thundering in her ears. It wasn't the most romantic of proposals, but she had to bite her lower lip to keep from blurting out her acceptance. It took half a minute for her to think rationally.

"I haven't said yes or no to moving in," she reminded him, pleased that she sounded like a sensible adult instead of a giddy teenager.

"I'm afraid I've gone about this in a clumsy fashion." His confident manner belied his words. "I've never asked a woman to marry me before. Especially not one I've known less than a month."

Hadley's brain scrambled to think logically. "And the reason you're rushing into marriage?"

"I'm not rushing into marriage," he corrected her with a wily grin. "I'm rushing into an engagement."

"Semantics." She waved away his explanation. "Are you sure you don't want to live together for a while and see how it goes?"

"I've already lived with you for a while and it's been terrific. I want to keep on living with you. I need you in my life. That's not going to change if we wait to get engaged. Right now your plan is to finish school and move to Houston. I want you to make a life with me in Royal instead."

Hadley clutched her reins in a white-knuckled grip and made no move toward the tempting ring box. "Are you sure this is what you want?"

From the way the light in his eyes dimmed, it wasn't the answer he'd hoped for, but he had to know her well enough to realize she wouldn't jump aboard his runaway freight train without thinking things through. After all, her career goals were designed to carry her far from Royal. And that was something she'd have to reconsider if she married him.

"Are you questioning whether I know my mind?" He lifted the enormous diamond ring from its nest of black velvet and caught her left hand. His eyes mesmerized her as he slid the ring on her finger. "I took a year off dating and spent the time thinking through what I wanted in a woman. I wouldn't have slept with you in Vail if I hadn't already made up my mind that you were special." Liam dismounted and handed off Buzzard's reins to one of the grooms.

"But marriage?" She stared at the ring, mesmerized by the diamond's sparkle.

Here was proof that Liam's proposal wasn't something impulsive and reckless. He'd come prepared to ask her to marry him. And yet he hadn't said anything about love.

"It's been on my mind constantly since we came back from Colorado."

Hearing she hadn't been the only one who'd felt the connection they'd established that snowy weekend eased her mind somewhat. She dismounted and surrendered Daisy to the groom as well. Her feet barely touched the dirt as she walked the short distance to Liam and took the hand he held outstretched.

He tugged her to him and lifted her chin with gentle fingers until their gazes met. "You fill my thoughts when we're apart and make me mad with longing to take you in my arms when we're together."

Liam's assertion awakened a deep, profound thrumming in her heart. "I know the feeling," she said, lifting onto her toes to offer him a single kiss. "I'd better get back to Maggie."

He wrapped a strong arm around her waist and held her snug against his muscular chest. "Will you stay tonight?"

"I can't. I'm having dinner with Kori."

"Afterward?"

She laughed and danced beyond his reach. "I've been neglecting the other guy in my life so I'm going to sleep with him."

"That guy better be Waldo," he growled, but his eyes sparkled with amusement below lowered brows.

"I don't have time for anyone else."

"Bring him with you when you come back. It's time you both settled permanently at the ranch house."

Engagement. Moving in. It was all happening so fast. Her heart hammered against her ribs in a panicked rhythm. All too aware she hadn't actually agreed to marry Liam, despite accepting his ring, she opened her mouth, but her thoughts were too scattered to summon words. He might have been considering this move for a while, but for her this development was brand-new and she needed to think things through.

One of Liam's ranch hands approached, citing a problem with a mare, and Hadley took the opportunity to slip away. As she wove through the connected barns on her way back to the ranch offices, her mood shifted from giddy to concerned. She might not have said yes to marriage, but she'd accepted his ring and kept her doubts to herself.

What had happened to being practical? Falling in love with Liam for starters. How was she supposed to think straight when the man made her feel like it was the Fourth of July, Thanksgiving and Christmas all rolled into one perfect holiday?

Thank goodness she was having dinner with Kori. Talking to her best friend would help sort things out.

Kori held Hadley's engagement ring mere inches from her nose and scrutinized the diamond. "You're not seriously thinking about marrying him, are you?"

"Well, I haven't said no." Hadley wasn't sure why her friend had done such a complete turnaround. "What's changed since last week when you told me to go for it?"

"Sex, yes." Kori regarded her friend as if she'd sprouted a second head as she opened the oven and removed her famous shepherd's pie. The succulent aroma of meat and savory gravy filled the kitchen. "Marriage, no."

Hadley held the plates while Kori filled them. Her friend's unexpected reaction to Liam's proposal was disheartening. "You're right. It's moving too fast."

"For you, yes." Kori and Scott had taken about a month to decide they wanted to be together forever. But they'd spent four years planning and saving money for their wedding.

"What if it feels right?" Hadley set the plates on the table while Kori followed with the salad.

"Did Noah feel right?"

Noah had been about safety. She'd been second-guessing her decision to change careers and had been worried about money. The notion of marrying a stable man had taken that burden off her shoulders.

"At the time." Hadley had no trouble admitting the truth of her failing. In the last five years she'd done a lot of soul-searching to understand why she'd failed to see that Noah was more interested in a mother for his children than a partner for life.

Kori nodded. "You are the most practical person I know until a single guy comes along needing help with his kids and you get all wrapped up in the idea of being a family."

It was her Achilles' heel, and she was wise enough to avoid putting herself in situations like the one with Noah. Like the one with Liam. As much as Hadley needed to hear Kori's blunt summary of her shortcomings, she wanted to protest that things with Liam were different. But were they?

Kori regarded her with a sympathetic expression while she topped off their wineglasses. "I know this isn't what you want to hear."

"You aren't saying anything I haven't thought a hundred times in the last month. I don't know why I do this. It's not like I didn't have a perfectly normal childhood. My parents are happily married, rarely fight and support me in everything I do."

"Don't be so hard on yourself. You are a born caretaker and one of the most nurturing people I know. It's in your nature to get overly invested, which is why you hated teaching a class of thirty kids. You might make a difference with one or two, but it's hard to give each child the sort of attention they need." Kori hit the problem squarely on the head. "Being a guidance counselor suits you so much better."

"I know." Hadley sighed. "But none of this helps me with what to do about Liam's marriage proposal. I really do love him."

"You haven't known him very long."

Hadley couldn't believe Kori of all people would use that argument. "Not directly, but I saw a lot of him ten years ago when I was barrel racing. I had a crush on him then. He was always nice to me. Never made me feel like I was going to be his next conquest." And for Liam, that was saying something.

"Because you weren't that sort of girl," Kori reminded her. "You told me while your friends dated extensively you weren't interested in boys, only horses."

"I was interested in Liam."

"Let me guess. He didn't know you existed?"

"At first, but toward the end of my last show season, that changed. I used to compete with his on-and-off girlfriend, and he'd sometimes show up to watch her. Most of the time I beat her, and he started congratulating me on my rides. At first I thought he was doing it to make her mad, but then I realized he meant it. One thing about Liam, he was always a horseman first and everything else came after."

"So things were warming up between you. What happened?"

"Anna was my best friend at the time, and she had a huge thing for him."

"But he liked you?"

Hadley shrugged. "He was way out of my league."

"What would you have done if he'd made a play for you?"

"Freaked out in true teenage fashion." Hadley trailed off as she recalled how much more intense her emotions had been in those days. Every problem had seemed crippling. Her success had sent her straight into orbit. "I'd never had a crush on anyone before, and Liam was older by a couple years and had a lot of experience. I told myself he couldn't possibly be interested in me that way."

"But you hoped he might be?"

"Sure, but it was complicated."

"Because of Anna?"

"Yes." Hadley hadn't told anyone the story behind Anna's accident. Ashamed that her friend was paralyzed as a result of something Hadley had said in a moment of anger, she'd punished herself all these years by avoiding something she loved: horses. "It bugged her that he'd go out of his way to comment on my rides but didn't notice her at all."

"What did she expect? That you'd tell him to stop being nice to you?" At Hadley's shrug, her friend sighed. "You should've told her to go to hell."

"I did something so much worse, and as a consequence my best friend lost the use of her legs."

Kori's eyes widened. "You need to tell me the whole story."

Haley killed the last of the wine in her glass and refilled from the bottle. "It was July and Wade Ranch was throwing a huge party at their stalls in the show barn to promote one of their stallions. Anna had been flirting with Liam for a month and was convinced he was finally showing interest when he invited her to the celebration. She dragged me along because she didn't want to go alone and then promptly ditched me to go hang with Liam. I lost track of her and spent the night hanging out with some of the other barrel racers.

"It was getting late and Anna didn't want to leave, so I arranged to get a lift with someone else. A little before we took off, I went to check on Lolita for the last time to make sure she had water and because being with her calmed me down. I was mad at Anna for chasing a guy who didn't act like he was into her."

"Because if he had been into her she wouldn't have had to chase him."

"Right." Several girls at the party had poked fun at Anna for thinking Liam could possibly be interested in her. "So, there I was in the stall with Lolita and guess who appears."

"Liam?" Kori said his name with such relish that Hadley had to smile.

"Liam. At first I thought maybe Anna was looking for me and got Liam to help her, but turns out he'd just followed me."

"Where was Anna?"

"I don't know. And really, for a little while, I didn't care. Liam and I talked about my upcoming ride the next day and he offered me advice for how to take a little time off my turns. I was grateful for the feedback and when I told him that, he said that if I won, I could take him out to dinner with my prize money."

"He asked you out?"

"I guess." Even now doubt clouded Hadley's tone. Even with Liam's engagement ring on her finger, she had a hard time believing that he'd been the slightest bit interested in her. She'd been so plain and uninteresting compared with his other girlfriends.

"You guess?" Kori regarded her in bemusement. "Of course he did."

Hadley shrugged. "Like I said, he was nice to a lot of people."

"But you had to suspect he wouldn't have tracked you to Lolita's stall if he wasn't interested in you."

"I could barely hope he liked me. I was excited and terrified. His reputation was something I wasn't sure I could deal with. He dated extensively." She put air quotes around *dated*. "I was eighteen and I'd never really been kissed."

"So did you win and go to dinner with him?"

"I won, but we never went out. Anna rode after I did the next day and had her accident."

"You haven't explained how that was your fault."

"Anna overheard Liam and I talking about dinner and me agreeing to his terms. She interrupted us and told me she was leaving and if I wanted a ride I'd better come with her. Considering I'd been ready to go an hour earlier, her demand seemed pretty unreasonable. I was tempted to tell her I'd already made other arrangements, but she was obviously upset so I agreed to head out."

"She was jealous that Liam had asked you out."

"That's what I figured, but on the way to the car I tried to explain to her that he was just helping me out with my riding."

"And she didn't believe you."

"No. She'd figured out I liked him and accused me of going behind her back. When I denied it, she went ballistic. Said that the only reason he noticed me was because I beat his girlfriend and that I wasn't his type. She insisted I would be the laughingstock of the barn if I kept believing he would ever want to date me."

"Sounds like things she should have been telling herself."

While Hadley agreed with Kori, at the time, each word had struck like a fist. "I wish I hadn't been so surprised by her attack. If I'd been able to stay calm, I might have been able to reason with her. But what she was saying were the same things that had been running through my head. To hear them from my best friend... I was devastated."

"So you didn't tell her she was the one who was acting like an idiot?"

"No." And now they'd arrived at the part of the story Hadley was most ashamed of. "I told her that if Liam only noticed me because of my riding she was out of luck. The way she rode, no wonder he had no idea who she was."

"Ouch."

Hadley winced. "Not my finest moment. And for the last ten years I've regretted those words."

"But it sounds like she was asking to have the truth served up to her."

"Maybe, but she was my best friend. I should have been more understanding. And because of what I said, the next day she pushed too hard and fell badly. So, now you see. If I'd not let my temper get the best of me, Anna never would have tried to prove she was the better rider and wouldn't have fallen and broken her back."

"And you haven't ridden since."

"No." It was a small sacrifice to make for being a bad

friend. "Until today. And now I'm engaged to the guy who came between Anna and me with tragic results."

"And I can tell you still aren't guilt free over moving on. So, as your best friend of seven years, I give you permission to get on with your life and stop beating yourself up over something you said to your friend who was acting like a greedy bitch a decade ago." Kori lifted her wineglass and held it out to Hadley.

Pushing aside all reluctance, Hadley picked up her glass and gently clinked it with Kori's. The crystalline note rang in the dining nook, the sound proclaiming an end to living in the past and the beginning of her bright future.

She'd given enough time and energy to her mistakes. She deserved to be happy, and being Liam's wife, becoming a family with him and Maggie, was the perfect way to spend the rest of her life.

Liam sat on the couch in the den, using one hand to scroll through the report Nolan's investigator had sent him regarding Margaret Garner while cradling a snugly swaddled Maggie in his other arm. She'd been fussy and agitated all day, and her appetite had waned. Hadley had noticed Maggie's temperature was slightly elevated and Liam was glad she was scheduled for a follow-up visit with her pediatrician tomorrow. Maggie continued to show signs of jaundice, and this had both Liam and Hadley concerned.

As a counterpoint to Liam's agitation over Maggie's health issues, Waldo lay on the sofa back directly behind Liam's head, purring. Although he'd grown up believing that cats belonged in barns, keeping the mouse population under control, he'd grown fond of Hadley's fur ball and had to concede that the feline had a knack for reading moods and providing just the right companionship. Just yesterday Liam had been irritated by a particularly demanding client, and Waldo had spent a hilarious ten minutes playing with one of Hadley's ponytail holders, cheering him up.

The only member of his family not sitting on the den's sofa was Hadley. After dinner she'd gone upstairs to call her parents and tell them about the engagement. They'd been on a cruise several days ago when Liam had popped the question and hadn't been immediately available to receive their daughter's news. Hadley was concerned that they'd view the engagement as moving too fast, and Liam had suggested that they take Maggie to Houston this weekend so everyone could meet.

With an effort, Liam brought his attention back to the report. Despite only spending four days on the job, the investigator had built a pretty clear picture of Maggie's mom. Margaret Garner had worked at home as a freelance illustrator and had a pretty limited social life. She'd dated rarely, and her friends had husbands and children who kept them busy. So busy, in fact, that none of them had had a clue that Margaret was pregnant. Nor had there been any contact between her and Kyle after their weeklong affair. The investigator hadn't been able to determine how the two had met, but after digging into Margaret's financials, he'd figured out when the fling had happened.

Margaret's perfectionism and heavy workload explained why she hadn't gone out much, but a couple of her friends had known Margaret since college and confided that they thought Margaret might have had some depression issues. From what the investigator could determine, she'd never sought medical help for that or gone to see a doctor when she'd discovered she was pregnant.

"Well, that's done," Hadley announced, her voice heavy as she crossed the room and settled onto the couch beside him.

"How did it go with your parents?"

"They were surprised." Her head dropped onto his shoulder. She'd been anxious about how the conversation would go all through dinner. Hadley was an only child and from her description of them, Liam got the impression they didn't exactly approve of some of the choices she'd made in the last few years. Especially when she'd quit teaching and moved to Royal in order to get her master's degree.

"What are you working on?"

"I had an investigator look into Margaret Garner's background."

"You hired an investigator? Why?" She peered more closely at the report on his computer screen.

"Nolan suggested it."

"Who is Nolan?"

"Nolan Dane is a family law attorney I hired."

"You hired a lawyer?"

Liam realized he probably should have shared his plans with her regarding Maggie before this, but hadn't anticipated that she'd be surprised. "Because I'm seeking custody of Maggie."

"Have you told your brother?"

"Kyle hasn't responded to my messages about Maggie yet."

Hadley sat up and turned on the cushions to face him. "Don't you think you should talk to him before you make such a big decision regarding his daughter?"

"I think it's obvious from the fact that it's been three weeks and I haven't heard from him that he's not in a place where he can be a father. Either he's overseas and unavailable or he's choosing not to call me back. Whichever it is, Maggie deserves parents who can always be there for her." He studied her expression with a hint of concern. "I thought you'd be on board with this. After all, you love Maggie as much as I do and have to admit we make terrific parents."

Her brows came together. "I guess I thought we'd be great with kids someday. As soon as I accepted that Maggie was your brother's daughter, I guess I thought she'd end up with him."

"Are you trying to tell me you can't see yourself as Maggie's mother?"

"Not at all. I love her..." But it was obvious that Hadley was grappling with something.

"Then what's going on?"

"I was just wondering how long you'd been thinking about this." Her tone had an accusatory edge he didn't understand.

"I've been considering what's best for Maggie since Diane Garner left her on my doorstep."

"And have you thought about what's best for your brother?"

Liam struggled for patience in the face of her growing hostility. "I'm thinking about the fact that he's a navy SEAL and likely to be called to duty at any time. He's not married and lives on the East Coast, far from family. Who is going to take care of Maggie while he's gone for weeks, maybe months at a time?" Liam met Hadley's gaze and didn't care for the indictment he glimpsed in her beautiful blue eyes. "I think Maggie would be better off here with us."

"He's not married." She spoke deliberately as if determined to make a point. "So he's not the best person to raise Maggie."

"He's a career military man with no family support," Liam corrected her, unsure why she wasn't agreeing with him. "How often will he miss a school event? How likely is it he'll be around for her first steps, first words, first... everything."

"You're not married, either," Hadley pointed out, her voice barely audible.

"But I'm engaged."

"Is that why you proposed?"

"What do you mean?"

"Obviously a married couple would be a stronger candidate in a custody battle."

"Sure." Why deny it? She wasn't a fool, and she knew him well enough to suspect he'd want to put forth the strongest case for Maggie.

However, the instant the admission was out, Hadley's whole demeanor transformed. All trace of antagonism vanished. She sagged in defeat.

Liam rushed to defend his rationale. "I'd like to point out that I've never asked any woman to marry me before you," he continued, more determined than ever to convince Hadley how much he needed her. "I want us to spend the rest of our lives together. With Maggie. As a family."

"I am such an idiot."

"I don't understand." He'd missed her jump in logic. "Why do you think you're an idiot?"

"Because it's just like Noah all over again."

"Noah?" The guy who'd broken her heart? "That's absurd. I asked you to marry me. He didn't."

"He said he wanted us to be together, too." Hadley shot to her feet and backed away, but her eyes never left Liam. "Only what he wanted was someone to take care of his kids and his house. Someone to be there when he got home at the end of the day and in his bed at night."

"You don't seriously think I proposed to you simply because I wanted you to fill a role." In order to keep Maggie slumbering peacefully, Liam kept his volume low, but made sure his outrage came through loud and clear.

"Everyone is right. It happened too fast." Hadley covered her mouth with her fingertips as a single tear slid down her cheek.

The sight of it disturbed him. He was fast losing control

of this situation and had no idea how to fix it. "Everyone? You mean your parents?"

"And my best friend, Kori. Not to mention the look on Candace's face when she found out."

"So what if our engagement happened fast?" Marrying Hadley meant both she and Maggie would stay with him at Wade Ranch. "That doesn't mean my motives are anything like you're painting them to be."

She pulled off her engagement ring and extended it to him. "So if I give this back to you and say I want to wait until I'm done with school to discuss our future, you'd be okay with it."

Liam made no move to take the ring back. Gripped by dismay, he stared at her, unable to believe that she was comparing him to some loser who'd used her shamelessly and broken her heart five years earlier.

"You're overreacting."

"Am I?" She crossed her arms over her chest. "When you proposed, you never told me you loved me."

No, he hadn't. He'd known he couldn't live without her, but he'd been consumed with winning custody of Maggie and afraid that Hadley would receive a job offer in Houston that would cement her plans for the future. He hadn't been thinking about romance or love when he'd proposed.

"That was wrong of me and I'm sorry. But I did tell you that I couldn't imagine life without you."

She shook her head. "You said you needed me in your life. That should've warned me that there was more motivating you than love."

"What does it matter what motivated me when it all comes down to how much we want to be together and how committed we are to being a family?"

"I really want that," she said, coming forward to set the engagement ring on the end table. "But I can't be in a relationship with you and know that your reasons for being in it are based on something besides love."

A lifetime of suppressed heartache at his mother's abandonment kept Liam from speaking as Hadley reached past him and disengaged her cat from his snug nest. Waldo's purring hadn't ceased during their argument, and Liam felt a chill race across his skin at the loss of the cat's warmth. It wasn't until she began to leave the room that he realized his mistake.

"Don't leave." He pushed aside his laptop and pursued Hadley into the hallway. "Hadley, wait."

She'd reached the entryway and slipped her coat off the hook. "I think it will be better if Waldo and I move back to my apartment. I'll be back in the morning to take care of Maggie." She didn't point out that the new nanny was set to start work in four days, but Liam was all too aware that he was on the verge of losing her forever.

"Maybe you're right and we moved too fast," he said. "But don't think for one second that I've changed my mind about wanting to spend the rest of my life with you." He extended his hand to catch her arm and stop her from leaving, but she sidestepped him, the unresisting cat clutched to her chest.

"I think it would be better for both of us if we focused on our individual futures. I have to finish school. You have a custody case to win. Once things settle down we can reconnect and see how we feel."

"If you think I'm going to agree to not see you for the next few months you've got it wrong."

"Of course we'll see each other." But her words weren't convincing. She set down the cat. Waldo stretched and wrapped himself around her legs while she donned her coat. Then, picking up her purse and the cat, Hadley opened the front door. "But I'm going to be crazy once classes start again, and you've got a couple hundred cattle set to give birth. Let's give ourselves a couple weeks to see where we're at."

"You're not going to be able to brush me off that easily," he growled as she slipped through the front door and pulled it closed behind her, leaving him and Maggie alone in the enormous, echoing Victorian mansion.

Twelve

Hadley was still reeling from déjà vu as she let herself into her apartment and set Waldo on the floor. The silver tabby's warmth had been a comfort as she'd sped through the early-evening darkness toward her tiny apartment.

How could she have been so stupid as to let herself get blinded by love a second time? So much for being five years older and wiser. She was obviously no less desperate; otherwise she wouldn't have become Liam's convenient solution the way she'd been Noah's. Honestly, what had happened to her common sense?

With her emotions a chaotic mess, Hadley looked for something in her apartment to occupy her, but after straightening a few pillows, dusting and running the vacuum, she ran out of tasks. While water boiled for a cup of tea, she wished her classes had resumed. At least then she'd have a paper to write or a test to study for. Something to occupy her thoughts and keep her mind off Liam.

She could call Kori and pour her heart out. Hadley rejected the idea as soon as it occurred to her. She wasn't ready to tell anyone that she'd screwed up again. The injury to her pride was still too fresh. Not to mention the damage to her confidence. As for the pain in her heart, Hadley could scarcely breathe as she considered all she'd lost tonight. Not just Liam, but Maggie as well.

Would it have been so bad to marry Liam and become

Maggie's mom? The whole time she'd been falling in love with Liam, she'd thought he and Maggie were a package deal. And then came their trip to Colorado. When she'd decided to believe him about his brother being Maggie's dad, letting her heart lead for a change hadn't felt one bit scary. She'd assumed Kyle would eventually come to Wade Ranch and take responsibility for Maggie. It never occurred to her that Liam intended to fight his brother for custody and that he might propose in order to appear to be the better candidate.

Desperate for a distraction from her turbulent thoughts, Hadley carried the hot tea to her small desk and turned on the computer. Before she'd considered her actions, she cued up the internet and impulsively ventured on to a popular social media site. Her fingers tapped out Noah's name and she pushed Enter before she could change her mind.

In seconds his page appeared and her heart gave a little jump as she stared at the photo of him and his kids that he used as his profile picture. Five years had gone by. Peter and Nikki were eight and seven now. They looked happy in their father's arms. Noah's wife wasn't in the shot, and Hadley searched through some of his other photos to see if she showed up anywhere. There were pictures of her with both kids, but none of her with Noah. Were they still married? Nothing in his profile information gave her a clue.

Feeling more than a little stalkerish, Hadley searched for Anna, but found no sign of her onetime friend. She almost left the website, inclined to switch to something with less potential for heartache, when she decided to search for Anna's sister, Char. And there she found Anna. Only she wasn't Anna Johnson any more. She was Anna Bradley now. A happily married woman with two beautiful girls.

Hadley stared at the photos in numb disbelief. This is the woman she'd been feeling guilty about for ten years? Anna hadn't wallowed in her misfortune. She hadn't sat around letting life pass her by. She'd gone to college in Dallas, become an engineer, gotten married and was busy raising a two- and a four-year-old.

It was as if the universe had reached out a hand and smacked Hadley on the back of the head and yelled, *snap out of it*. Noah had moved forward with his life. He had his kids and seemed to be in a good place with his wife or ex-wife. Anna was thriving with a career and family. Apparently Hadley was the only one stuck in limbo.

With revelations pouring over her like ice water, Hadley shut down the computer and picked up a notebook and a pen. It was time for her to stop dwelling on what had happened in the past and to consider how she envisioned her future. What was her idea of a perfect career? Where did she want to live? Was the love in her heart strong enough to overcome her doubts and fears?

Liam entered the pediatrician's office and spotted Hadley seated by the wall, Maggie's carrier on the chair beside her. Overnight the baby's temperature had risen, and the concern radiating from Hadley caused a spike in his anxiety.

"How is she?" he asked as he sat beside Maggie and peered in her carrier.

"A little bit worse than she was when I arrived this morning. She wouldn't eat and seems listless. I'm glad we had this appointment scheduled today."

Hadley was obviously distraught, and Liam badly wanted to offer her the comfort of his embrace, but yesterday she hadn't believed him when he'd told her there was more to his proposal than his determination to seek custody of Maggie. What made him think that a miracle had occurred overnight to change her mind?

"Do you think the jaundice is causing this?"

"More likely the jaundice is a symptom of something more serious."

"Damn it." The curse vibrated in his chest as anxiety flared. He stared down at the sleeping baby. "I can't lose her."

"Liam, you're not going to lose her." Hadley reached across Maggie's carrier and set her fingers on his upper arm.

The light contact burned through him like a wildfire, igniting his hope for a future with her. She loved him. The proof was in her supportive tone and her desire to reassure him. But as he reached to cover her hand with his, she withdrew. When she spoke again, her voice had a professional crispness.

"She's going to be fine."

He hated the distance between them. He'd been wrong to propose to her as part of a scheme to win custody of Maggie. Even though it hadn't been his only reason for asking her to marry him, she'd been right to feel as if he'd treated her no better than Noah.

But how could he convince her to give him another chance when she'd rejected everything he'd already said and done? As with the subject of Maggie's paternity, she was either going to believe him or she wasn't. She'd been burned before, and her lack of trust demonstrated that she hadn't yet moved on. He'd have to be patient and persistent. Two things he was known for when it came to horses, but not in his personal life.

"Hadley, about what happened last night—"

A nurse appeared in the waiting room and called Maggie's name before Hadley could respond. Liam ground his teeth as he and Hadley followed the nurse into an exam room. He refocused his attention on Maggie as the nurse weighed and measured her. After it was determined that her temperature had climbed to 102, the nurse left to fetch Dr. Stringer.

Liam's tension ratcheted upward during the wait. Hadley sat beside him with Maggie cradled in her arms. She'd fixed her gaze on the door to the hall as if she could summon the doctor by sheer will.

After a wait that felt like hours but was less than ten minutes, Maggie's doctor appeared. Dr. Stringer made a quick but thorough examination of his patient, returned her to Hadley's arms and sat down, his expression solemn.

"I'm concerned that she's running a temperature and that the jaundice hasn't gone away after the phototherapy treatments," Dr. Stringer said. "I'd like to draw blood and recheck her bilirubin levels. If they continue to remain high we may want to look at the possibility of doing a blood transfusion."

Liam felt rather than heard Hadley's sharp intake of breath. She had leaned her shoulder against his as the doctor had spoken. The seriousness of Maggie's medical condition was a weight Liam was glad not to have to bear alone.

"Maggie is a rare blood type," Liam said. "AB negative. Is that going to pose a problem finding donors?"

The doctor shook his head. "Not at all. In fact, where O is the universal donor blood type, AB is the universal recipient. But let's not get ahead of ourselves. I'm going to have the nurse draw some blood and then we'll see where we're at."

Maggie's reaction to the blood draw was not as vigorous as Liam expected it to be, and he took that as a sign that she was even sicker than she appeared. This time as they sat alone in the exam room, Liam reached for Hadley's hand. Her fingers were ice cold, but they curved to hold fast to his.

Their second wait was longer, but no less silent. Liam's

heart thumped impatiently, spreading unease through every vein. Beside him, Hadley, locked in her own battle with worry, gripped his hand and stared down at Maggie. Both of them had run out of reassuring things to say.

The door opened again and Dr. Stringer entered. "Looks like it's not her bilirubin levels that are causing the problem," he said, nothing about his manner suggesting this was good news.

"Then what's going on?" Liam asked.

"We're seeing a high level of white blood cells that points to infection. Because of the jaundice and the fact that she's a preemie, I'd like you to take Maggie to the hospital for further testing. I've already contacted my partner, Dr. Davison. He's on call at the hospital today and will be waiting for you."

"The hospital?" Hadley sounded stunned. "It's that serious?"

"At this point we don't know, but I would rather err on the side of caution."

Liam nodded. "Then we'll head right over."

Hadley sat in the passenger side of Liam's Range Rover as he drove to the hospital and silently berated herself for being a terrible caregiver.

"This isn't your fault," Liam said, demonstrating an uncanny knack for knowing what she was thinking.

"You don't know that."

"She only just recently started showing signs of an infection."

"But we don't know how long this has been brewing. You heard the doctor. He said it could have been coming on slowly for a long time. What if she was sick before we went to Colorado and then we walked to town and back? Maybe that's when things started."

"We can't know for sure and you'll make yourself crazy if you keep guessing."

"I should never have..." She trailed off, biting her lip to stifle the rest of the sentence.

"Should never have what?" Liam demanded, taking his eyes off the road to glance her way.

She answered in a rush. "Slept with you."

"Why? Because by doing that you stopped being a good nanny?" He snorted derisively.

Hadley shifted away from his irritation and leaned her head against the cool window. "Maggie was my responsibility. I got distracted."

"She's my responsibility, too," he reminded her. "I'm just as much at fault if something happens to her. You know, one of these days you should stop blaming yourself for every little thing that goes wrong."

With a shock, Hadley realized that Liam was right. She'd taken responsibility for other people's decisions, believing if she'd been a better friend, Anna wouldn't have gotten hurt, and if she'd been more affectionate with Noah or acted more like a parent to his children instead of their nanny, he might not have gone back to his ex-wife.

"It's a habit I should break," she said, her annoyance diminished. "It's really not anyone's fault she's sick. Like the doctor said, her birth wasn't routine. The infection could have been caused by any number of things."

Neither spoke again, but the silence was no longer charged by antagonism. Hadley cast several glances in Liam's direction, wishing she hadn't overreacted last night after finding out Liam intended to seek custody of Maggie. But she'd gone home and filled two sheets of paper with a list of everything that made her happy. It had taken her half a page before she'd begun to break free of the mental patterns she'd fallen into. But it was the last two items that told the real story.

Horses.

Liam.

That it had taken her so long to admit what she needed in her life to be truly happy was telling.

Liam dropped her and Maggie off at the emergency entrance and went to park. Hadley checked in at reception and was directed to the waiting room. She was told someone would come down from pediatrics to get them soon.

To Hadley's relief they only had to wait ten minutes. Liam never even had a chance to sit down before they were on their way to a private room in Royal Memorial's brand-new west wing.

A nurse entered the room while Hadley lifted Maggie from her carrier. "Hello, my name is Agnes and I'll be taking care of Maggie while she's here."

"It's nice to meet you." Hadley followed Agnes's directions and placed Maggie in the bassinet. It was hard to step away from the baby and let the nurse take over, but Hadley forced herself to join Liam by the window.

Liam gave her a tight smile. "She's in good hands."

"I know." Hadley was consumed by the need for Liam's arms around her. But she'd relinquished all rights to his reassurances last night when she'd given back his engagement ring.

The nurse took Maggie's vitals and hooked her up to an IV.

"Because she's not yet four weeks," Agnes began, "we're going to start her on antibiotics right away. It may take twenty-four to forty-eight hours to get the lab results back, so we'd like to take this precaution. The good news is that it hasn't seemed to affect her lungs. That's always a concern with a premature baby." Agnes offered a reassuring smile before continuing. "Dr. Davison will be by in a little while to talk to you."

"Thank you," Liam said while Hadley crossed to Maggie.

"She looks even tinier hooked up to the IV."

Liam came to stand beside her and stared down at Maggie. A muscle jumped in his jaw. His eyes had developed a haunted look. Suddenly it was Hadley's turn to offer comfort.

"She's going to be fine."

"Thank you for being here," he said. "It's…"

She'd never know what he intended to say because a man in a white lab coat entered the room with Agnes at his heels.

"Good morning, I'm Dr. Davison. I've spoken with Dr. Stringer and he filled me in on what's been going on. I'm sure you're anxious to hear about the tests we ran on Maggie," The doctor met each of their gazes in turn before shifting his attention to the infant. "What we're looking at is a blood infection. That's what's causing the fever, her jaundice and her listlessness."

A knot formed in Hadley's chest. She gripped Liam's forearm for stability. "Is it serious?"

"It can be. But Maggie is in good hands with us here at Royal Memorial. I'm sure she'll make a full recovery. The sooner she gets treatment the better the outcome. We've already started her on antibiotics, and we're going to monitor her for the next couple days while we run a battery of tests to determine what's causing the infection."

"How long will she be here?" Liam gave Hadley's fingers a gentle squeeze.

"Probably not more than three days. If there's bacteria in her blood, she'll be on antibiotics for three weeks and you'll be bringing her in for periodic checkups."

"Thank you, Dr. Davison." Liam extended his hand to the pediatrician and appeared less overwhelmed than he had before the doctor's arrival.

"Yes, thank you." Hadley summoned a smile.

Dr. Davison turned to the nurse. "Agnes, would you prepare Maggie for a lumbar puncture?"

"Certainly, Dr. Davison." She smiled at Liam and Hadley. "We have some paperwork at the nurses' station for you to fill out," she said. "We'll need just a few minutes for the spinal tap and then you can come back and be with Maggie."

Hadley tensed, intending to resist being evicted for the procedure, but then she remembered that she was the nanny, nothing more. She'd given up her rights when she'd given Liam back his ring.

When they stepped into the hallway, Hadley turned to Liam. "I should go."

"Go?" he echoed, his expression blank, eyes unfocused. "Go where?"

"I don't really belong here." As much as that was true in a practical sense, she couldn't shake a feeling of responsibility to Maggie and to him.

Foolishness. If anyone besides Liam had hired her, she wouldn't have let herself get personally involved. She'd never slept with any of her other clients, either. Even with Noah she hadn't stepped across that line. They'd been close, but something about sleeping with him with his children down the hall hadn't sat well with her. And right before the weekend they were supposed to go away and be together for the first time was when Noah decided to go back to his ex-wife.

"Maggie needs you," Liam countered. "You can't leave her now."

"I'm her nanny." It hurt to admit it, but Hadley knew that after what had happened between her and Liam, she needed to start pulling back. "What she needs is her family. Why don't you call her grandmother?"

"You mean the woman who left her with me and hasn't demonstrated any grandmotherly concern since?"

Hadley was torn. Her presence wasn't needed while Maggie was at the hospital. The nurses would see to it that the baby was well tended. Liam could give her all the love and snuggling she required.

"I'm sorry that Maggie's mother died and her grandmother is so far away, but I can't be here for you and for her in this way. She's in good hands with the nurses and with you. I've already gotten too involved. I can't keep pretending like nothing has changed." Hadley turned in the direction of the elevator so Liam wouldn't see her tears.

He caught her arm before she could take a step. "I'm sorry, too," he murmured in her ear, his breath warm against her temple. "I never meant for any of this to hurt you."

And then he set her free. Gutted and empty, she walked away without glancing back.

Liam sat on the couch in Maggie's hospital room. A nurse had appeared half an hour ago to take Maggie's temperature and change her diaper. When she'd completed her tasks, she'd dimmed the lights and left Liam in semidarkness. It was a little past six. He'd skipped both lunch and dinner but couldn't bring himself to leave the room. He felt empty, but it wasn't because he was hungry. The hollowness was centralized in his chest. Loneliness engulfed him unlike anything he'd known before.

He hadn't felt this lost when Kyle left for the navy or when his grandfather had died. The ranch had provided abundant distractions to occupy him, and he'd thrown himself into building the business. That wasn't going to work this time.

He rarely felt sorry for himself, but in the eight hours since Hadley had taken off, he'd begun to realize the wrong turn his life had taken. The arrival of Maggie and Hadley had been the best thing that had ever happened to him. Acting as Maggie's caretaker had taught him the true meaning of the word *responsibility*. Up until now, he'd had people who did things for him. Staff, his grandfather, even the women he dated. While he didn't think of himself as selfish, he'd never had to put anyone's needs above his own.

But even as he'd patted himself on the back for championing Maggie's welfare, hadn't he ignored his brother's needs when he'd decided to seek custody of his niece? And Hadley's? How had he believed that being married to him was any sort of reward for her love and the sacrifice to her career that staying in Royal would require?

He'd played it safe, offered her an expensive ring and explained that he needed her and wanted her in his life. But he'd never once told her he was madly, passionately in love with her and that if she didn't marry him, he'd be heartbroken. Of course she'd felt underappreciated.

Liam thought about the nightmare he'd had after returning from Colorado. Sleeping alone for the first time in three nights had dragged powerful emotions from his subconscious. He could still recall the sharp pain in his chest left over by the dream, a child's hysterical panic as he'd chased his mother out of the house, pleading with her not to go.

By the time he'd awakened the next morning, there'd been nothing left of the disturbing dream but a lingering sense of uneasiness. He'd shoved the genie back into the bottle. Craving love only to have it denied him was not something he ever wanted to experience again. And so he'd only shown Hadley physical desire and made a superficial commitment without risking his heart.

She'd been right to leave him. He'd pushed her to ride again, knowing how devastated she'd been by her friend's accident. He'd badgered her to forgive herself for mistakes she'd made in the past without truly understanding how difficult that was for her. But worst of all, he'd taken her love and given nothing back.

Liam reached into his pocket and drew out the engagement ring. The diamonds winked in the dim artificial light. How many of his former girlfriends would have given it back? Probably none. But they would've been more interested in the expensive jewelry than the man who gifted it. Which explained why he'd chosen them in the first place. With women who wanted nothing more from him than pretty things and a good time, he never had to give of himself.

What an idiot he'd been. He'd stopped dating so his head would be clear when the right girl came along. And when she had, he'd thought to impress her with a trip to Vail and a big engagement ring. But Hadley was smart as well as stubborn. She was going to hold out for what really mattered: a man who loved her with all his heart and convinced her with words as well as deeds just how important she was to him.

Up until now, he hadn't been that man. And he'd lost her. But while she remained in Royal, he had a chance to show her how he truly felt. And that's exactly what he was going to do.

Thirteen

After abandoning Liam and Maggie at the hospital, Hadley took a cab home and spent the rest of the day on the couch watching a reality TV marathon. The ridiculous drama of overindulged, pampered women was a poor distraction from the guilt clawing at her for leaving Liam alone to cope with Maggie. Worry ate at her and she chided herself for not staying, but offering Liam comfort was a slippery slope. Already her emotions were far too invested.

At seven she sent Kori a text about getting a ride to Wade Ranch in the morning to pick up her car. She probably should have gone tonight, but felt too lethargic and even had a hard time getting off the couch to answer the door for the pizza delivery guy.

It took her friend an hour to respond to the text. Hadley forgot she hadn't told Kori yet about her broken engagement. Leave it to her to have the world's shortest engagement. It hadn't even lasted three days. With a resigned sigh, Hadley dialed Kori's number.

"So, what's going on that you left your car at Liam's?"

Kori's question unleashed the floodgates. Hadley began to sob. She rambled incoherently about Maggie being in the hospital and how she'd turned her back on Liam right when he needed her the most.

"I'm coming over."

"No. It's okay." Hadley blew her nose and dabbed at her eyes. "I'm fine."

"You are so not fine. Why didn't you tell me about this last night?"

"Because I wasn't ready to admit that I'd screwed up and fallen in love with the wrong man again. Honestly, why do I keep doing this to myself?"

"You didn't know he was the wrong guy until too late."

"It's because I jump in too fast. I get all caught up in his life and fall in love with the idea of being a family."

"I thought you said Liam hadn't told you that he planned to fight for custody of Maggie."

"Well…no."

"Then technically, you weren't planning on being a family with Liam and Maggie, but a couple with Liam."

"And eventually a family."

"Since eventually is in the future, I don't think that counts." Kori's voice was gentle but firm. "You love Liam. You told me you had a crush on him when you were a teenager. Isn't it possible that what you feel for him has nothing to do with seeing yourself as part of a family and everything to do with the fact that you're in love with him?"

"Sure." Did that make things better or worse? "But what about the fact that he asked me to marry him because he thought he would have a better chance to get custody if he was engaged?"

"I'm not really sure it's that straightforward," Kori said. "Liam Wade is a major catch. He's probably got dozens of women on speed dial that he's known a lot longer than you. Don't you wonder why he didn't ask one of them to marry him? I think he fell for you and is too afraid to admit it."

As tempting as it was to believe her friend's interpretation, Hadley knew it would just lead to more heartache. She couldn't spend the rest of her life wondering what if.

Kori's sigh filled Hadley's ear. "I can tell from your

silence that you don't agree. I'm sorry all this happened. You are such a wonderful person. You deserve the best guy in the world."

"And he's out there somewhere," Hadley said with what she hoped was a convincing amount of enthusiasm.

"What time do you want me to come get you tomorrow?"

"It doesn't matter." She figured Liam would stay at the hospital with Maggie until she was ready to go home, and that would give Hadley a chance to collect her things from the house without the risk of running into him.

"I'm meeting a client at eight. We can either go before or after."

"I guess I'd rather go early." The sooner she collected all her things, the sooner she could put all her mistakes behind her.

Maggie's new nanny was set to start the day after to-morrow, and Hadley doubted Dr. Davison would release her before that, so she didn't have to worry about see-ing Liam ever again. The thought sent a stabbing pain through her.

"How about seven?"

"That would be perfect," Hadley said and then switched to the less emotionally charged topic of their upcoming girls' night out.

After a few more minutes, Hadley hung up. It took about ten seconds to go back to thinking about Liam. How was Maggie doing? Had her test results come back yet? Liam must be frantic waiting to hear something.

She brought up the messaging app on her phone, but stopped as she realized what she was doing. Contacting Liam would undo what little peace she'd found during the afternoon. It might be agonizing to cut ties with Liam and Maggie, but in the long run it would be better for all of them.

Yet no matter how many times she reminded herself of that fact as the evening dragged on, she wasn't able to put the baby or Liam out of her mind. Finally, she broke down and sent Liam a text around ten thirty, then shut off her phone and went to bed. But sleep eluded her. Despite having reached out to Liam, she couldn't put concern aside.

Around six, Hadley awoke. Feeling sluggish, her thoughts a jittery mess, she dragged herself out of bed and climbed into the shower. The closer it got to Kori's arrival, the more out of sorts Hadley became. Despite how unlikely it was that she'd run into Liam, she couldn't stop the anxiety that crept up her spine and sent a rush of goose bumps down her arm. By the time Hadley eased into Kori's passenger seat, she was a ball of nerves.

"You okay?" Kori asked, steering the car away from Hadley's apartment building.

"Fine. I didn't sleep very well. I couldn't stop thinking about Maggie and wondering how she's doing."

"You should call or text Liam and find out. I don't think he would have a problem with you letting him know you're worried."

"I did last night. He never got back to me." Hadley sounded as deflated as she felt. What had she expected? That Liam would fall all over himself telling her how much he missed her and that he regretted letting her go?

"Oh," Kori said, obviously stumped for an answer. "Well, then to hell with him."

That made Hadley smile. "Yeah," she agreed with fake bravado. "To hell with him."

But she didn't really mean it. She didn't even know if Liam had received her text. His focus was 100 percent fixed on Maggie, as was right. He'd answer in due time.

Twenty minutes later, Kori dropped her off at Wade Ranch. Hadley was relieved that her car was the only one in the driveway. She wouldn't have to run into Liam and make awkward conversation.

As soon as Hadley opened the front door she was assailed by the mouthwatering scent of cinnamon and sugar. She followed her nose to the kitchen and found Candace putting caramel rolls into a plastic container. Forgetting her intention had been to pack her suitcase with the few belongings she'd brought to the ranch house and get out as soon as possible, Hadley succumbed to the lure of Candace's incomparable pastries and sat down on one of the stools next to the island, fixing the housekeeper with a hopeful gaze.

"Those smell incredible."

"I thought I'd take them over to Liam at the hospital and give him a break so he could come home and clean up."

"That's really nice of you."

"But now that you're here, maybe you could take them to him instead." Candace caught Hadley's grimace and frowned. "What's wrong?"

"I don't know that Liam is going to want to see me." At Candace's puzzled expression, Hadley explained, "We broke off our engagement and I left him all alone at the hospital yesterday." *After freaking out on him*, she finished silently.

"I don't understand. Did you have a fight?"

"Not exactly. It's more that we rushed into things. I mean, we've only known each other a short time, and who gets engaged after three weeks?"

"But you two were so much in love. And it is an engagement, after all. You'll have plenty of time to get to know each other while you plan your wedding."

Hadley couldn't bring herself to explain to Candace that Liam didn't love her and only proposed so he could improve his chances of gaining custody of Maggie. "It was all just too fast," she murmured.

"But what about Maggie? I'm sure that Liam would appreciate your support with her being in the hospital."

Nothing Hadley could say would be good enough to rationalize abandoning a sick baby, so she merely hung her head and stared at the veins of silver glinting in the granite countertop. "I'll take the caramel rolls to Liam," she said at last. "And maybe some coffee as well. He's sure to be exhausted."

Candace nodded in approval. "He'll like that."

While Candace sealed up the rolls, Hadley poured coffee into a thermos, wondering how she'd let herself get talked into returning to the hospital. Then she sighed. It hadn't taken much prompting from Candace. In fact, Hadley was happy for an excuse to visit.

"If you're afraid because things between you have happened too fast," Candace began, turning away to carry the empty caramel roll pan to the sink, "I think you should know that I've never seen Liam as happy as he is with you."

"He makes me happy, as well." Had she let a past hurt blind her to everything that was true and loving about Liam?

"Whatever stands between you two can't possibly be insurmountable if you choose to work together to beat it."

What if fear of being hurt again had led to her overreacting to Liam's desire to seek custody of Maggie? Was it possible that she'd misjudged him? Attributed motives to him that didn't exist, all because she couldn't trust her own judgment?

"You're probably right."

"Then maybe you two should consider being open with each other about what it is you want and how you can achieve it."

Hadley offered Candace a wry smile. "It sounds so easy when you say it."

"Being in love isn't always easy, but in my experience, it's totally worth the ride."

"And Liam is totally worth taking that ride with," Hadley agreed. "Perhaps it's time I stopped being afraid of telling him that."

"Perhaps it is."

* * *

Liam hovered over Maggie's bassinet as the nurse took her temperature. "Her appetite was better this morning," he said.

The nurse hadn't missed his anxious tone and gave him a reassuring smile. "Her temperature is down a couple degrees. Looks like the antibiotics are doing what they're supposed to."

While it wasn't a clean bill of health, at least Maggie's situation was trending in the right direction. "That's great news." He wished he could share the update with Hadley, but she'd made it clear yesterday that she needed distance. It cut deep that he'd driven her away.

"She's sleeping now," the nurse said. "Why don't you take the opportunity to get something to eat? From what I hear, you skipped dinner last night."

"I wasn't hungry."

"Well, you're not going to do your little girl any good if you get run-down and can't take care of her once she's ready to go home." The nurse gave him a stern look.

"Sure, you're right." But he couldn't bring himself to leave Maggie alone. "I'll go down to the cafeteria in a little while."

Once the nurse left, Liam brushed a hand through his hair, suddenly aware he was practically asleep on his feet. He hadn't been able to do more than snatch a couple naps during the night and could really use a cup of coffee. It occurred to him that he wasn't going to be able to keep this pace up for long, but he would never be able to forgive himself if Maggie got worse while he was gone.

A soft female voice spoke from the doorway. "How's she doing?"

Blinking back exhaustion, Liam glanced up and spied Hadley hovering in the hallway. From her apprehensive expression, she obviously expected him to throw her out.

"A little better."

"That's great. I hope it's okay that I came by."

"Sure." After yesterday, he could barely believe she'd come back. "Of course."

"I wasn't sure…" She looked around the room as if in search of somewhere to hide. "You didn't answer my text last night."

He rubbed his face to clear some of the blurriness from his mind. "You sent a text? I didn't get it."

"Oh." She held up a rectangular container and a silver thermos. "I brought you coffee and some of Candace's caramel rolls. She was going to come herself, but I had to pick up my car and was heading back this way…" She trailed off as if unnerved by his silence. "I can just leave them and go. Or I can stay with Maggie while you go home and shower or sleep. You don't look like you got any last night."

She didn't look all that refreshed, either. Of course she'd worried. He imagined her tossing and turning in her bed, plagued by concern for Maggie. It was in her nature to care even when it wasn't in her best interest to do so.

"I'm so sorry," he told her, his voice a dry rasp. "I should never have let you leave yesterday. We should have talked."

"No." She shook her head and took two steps toward him. "I should apologize. The way I acted yesterday was unforgivable. I should never have been thinking of myself when Maggie was so sick."

Liam caught her upper arms and pulled her close. He barely noticed the container of rolls bump against his stomach as he bent his head and kissed her firmly on the lips, letting his emotions overwhelm him. The aching tightness in his chest released as she gave a little moan before yielding her lips to his demand.

He let go of her arms and stroked his palms up her shoulders and beneath her hair, cupping her head so he could feast on her mouth. Time stood still. The hospital room fell away as he showed her the emotions he'd been keeping hidden. His fear, his need, his joy. Everything she made him feel. He gave it all to her.

"Liam." She breathed his name in wonder as he nuzzled his face into her neck.

"I love you." The words came so easily to him now. Gone were his defenses, stripped away by an endless, lonely night and his elation that she'd returned. He wasn't going to let her question his devotion ever again. "No, I adore you. And will do whatever it takes for as long as it takes for you to believe you are the only woman for me."

A smile of happiness transformed her. He gazed down into her overly bright eyes and couldn't believe how close he'd come to losing her.

"I love you, too," she replied, lifting on tiptoe to kiss him lightly on the lips.

"I rushed you because I was afraid your career would take you away, and I couldn't bear to lose you." Suddenly it was easy to share his fears with her, and from the way she regarded him, she understood what he'd been going through. "This time we'll take it slow," he promised. "I'm determined that you won't feel rushed into making up your mind about spending the rest of your life with me."

She gave a light laugh. "I don't need any time. I love you and I want to marry you. Together we are going to be a family. No matter what happens with Kyle, Maggie will always be like a daughter to us and a big sister to our future children."

"In that case." He fished the ring out of his pocket and dropped to one knee. "Hadley Stratton, love of my life, would you do me the honor of becoming my wife?"

She shifted the thermos beneath her arm and held out her left hand. "Liam Wade, loving you is the most wonderful thing that has ever happened to me. I can't wait for us to get married and live happily ever after."

He slipped the ring onto her finger and got to his feet. Bending down, he kissed her reverently on the lips. One kiss turned into half a dozen and both of them were out of breath and smiling foolishly when they drew apart.

"Kissing you is always delightful," she said, handing him the coffee. "And we really must do much more of that later, but right now my mouth has been watering over these caramel rolls for the last hour."

"You're choosing food over kissing me?"

"These are Candace's caramel rolls," she reminded him, popping the top on the container and letting the sugary, cinnamon smell fill the room.

"I get your point." He nodded, his appetite returning in a flash. "Let's eat."

The morning of her wedding dawned clear and mild. The winds that had buffeted the Texas landscape for the last week had calmed, and the weather forecasters were promising nothing but pleasant temperatures for several days to come.

Today at eleven o'clock she was marrying Liam in an intimate ceremony at the Texas Cattleman's Club. Naturally Kori was her matron of honor while Liam's best man would be Mac McCallum. Because the wedding was happening so fast, Hadley had opted for a white tulle skirt and sleeveless white lace top that showed a glimpse of her midriff. Since she was marrying a man she'd reconnected with less than a month earlier, Hadley decided to kick conventional to the curb and wear something trendy rather than a traditional gown.

Kori had lent her the white silk flower and crystal headpiece she'd worn at her wedding. Her something borrowed. She wore a pair of pearl-and-diamond earrings once owned by Liam's grandmother. Her something old. For her something blue and new, Hadley purchased a pair of bright blue cowboy boots.

The shock on her mother's face validated Hadley's choice, but it was the possessive gleam in Liam's eyes as she walked down the aisle at the start of the ceremony that assured her she'd been absolutely right to break the mold and let her true self shine.

"You look gorgeous," he told her as she took the hand he held out to her.

She stepped beside him and tucked her hand into the crook of his arm. "I'm glad you think so. I thought of you when I bought everything."

He led her toward the white arch where the minister waited. A harp played in the corner, the tune something familiar to weddings, but Hadley was conscious only of the tall man at her side and the sense of peace that filled her as the minister began to speak.

Swearing to love, honor and be true to Liam until the day she died was the easiest promise she'd ever had to make. And from the sparkle in his eyes as he slid the wedding ring onto her finger, he appeared just as willing to pledge himself completely to her.

At last the minister introduced them as husband and wife, and they led their guests into the banquet room that had been set up for the reception. Draped with white lights and tulle, the room had a romantic atmosphere that stopped Hadley's breath.

Flowers of every color filled the centerpieces on the tables. Because of the limited time for the preparations, Hadley had told the florist to pull together whatever he had. She'd carried a bouquet of orange roses and pink lilies, and Liam wore a hot-pink rose on his lapel.

"I had no idea it was going to be this gorgeous," she murmured.

"The only gorgeous thing in the room is you."

Hadley lifted onto her toes and kissed him. "And that's why I love you. You always know what makes me smile."

And so ended their last intimate moment as newlyweds for the next three hours as social demands kept them occupied with their guests. At long last they collected Maggie from her circle of admirers and headed back to Wade Ranch. Together they put her to bed and stood beside the crib watching her sleep.

"I meant to give this to you earlier but didn't get the chance." Liam extended a small flat box to her.

"What is it?"

"Open it and see."

Hadley raised the lid and peered down at the engraved heart-shaped pendant in white gold. She read the inscription, "Follow your heart. Mine always leads to the barn." She laughed. "I used to have a T-shirt with that on it."

"I remember." Liam lifted the necklace from the bed of black velvet and slipped it over her head. "You were wearing it the first time I saw you."

"That was more than ten years ago." Hadley was stunned. "How could you possibly remember that?"

"You'd be surprised what I remember about you."

She threaded her fingers through his hair and pulled him down for a kiss. "It's a lovely gift, but it no longer pertains."

"I thought you'd gotten past your guilt about your friend."

"I have." She smiled up at him. "But my heart no longer leads me to the barn. It leads me to you."

He bent down and swept her off her feet. "And that, Mrs. Wade, is the way it should be."

* * * * *

Don't miss a single installment of
TEXAS CATTLEMAN'S CLUB:
LIES AND LULLABIES
Baby secrets and a scheming sheikh rock Royal, Texas

COURTING THE COWBOY BOSS
by USA TODAY *bestselling author Janice Maynard*

LONE STAR HOLIDAY PROPOSAL
by USA TODAY *bestselling author Yvonne Lindsay*

NANNY MAKES THREE
by Cat Schield

THE DOCTOR'S BABY DARE
by USA TODAY *bestselling author Michelle Celmer*

THE SEAL'S SECRET HEIRS
by Kat Cantrell

A SURPRISE FOR THE SHEIKH
by Sarah M. Anderson

IN PURSUIT OF HIS WIFE
by Kristi Gold

A BRIDE FOR THE BOSS
by USA TODAY *bestselling author Maureen Child*

***

If you're on Twitter, tell us what you think of
Harlequin Desire! #harlequindesire

COMING NEXT MONTH FROM

Available February 2, 2016

#2425 His Forever Family
Billionaires and Babies • by Sarah M. Anderson
When caring for an abandoned baby brings Liberty and her billionaire boss Marcus closer, she must resist temptation. Her secrets could destroy her career and the chance to care for the foster child they are both coming to love...

#2426 The Doctor's Baby Dare
Texas Cattleman's Club: Lies and Lullabies
by Michelle Celmer
Dr. Parker Reese always gets what he wants, especially when it comes to women. When a baby shakes up his world, he decides he wants sexy nurse Clare Connelly... Will he have to risk his guarded heart to get her?

#2427 His Pregnant Princess Bride
Bayou Billionaires • by Catherine Mann
What starts as a temporary vacation fling for an arrogant heir to a Southern football fortune and a real-life princess becomes way more than they bargained for when the princess becomes pregnant!

#2428 How to Sleep with the Boss
The Kavanaghs of Silver Glen • by Janice Maynard
Ex-heiress Libby Parkhurst has nothing to lose when she takes a demanding job with Patrick Kavanagh, but her desire to impress the boss is complicated when his matchmaking family gives her a makeover that makes Patrick lose control.

#2429 Tempted by the Texan
The Good, the Bad and the Texan • by Kathie DeNosky
Wealthy rancher Jaron Lambert wants more than just one night with Mariah Stanton, but his dark past and their age difference hold him back. What will it take to push past his boundaries? Mariah's about to find out...

#2430 Needed: One Convenient Husband
The Pearl House • by Fiona Brand
To collect her inheritance, Eva Atraeus only has three weeks to marry. Billionaire banker Kyle Messena, the trustee of the will *and* her first love, rejects every potential groom...until he's the only one left! How convenient...

HDCNM0116

"You have to make a decision about attending the Hanson wedding."

Marcus groaned. He did not want to watch his former fiancée get married to the man she'd cheated on him with. Unfortunately, to some, his inability to see the truth about Lillibeth until it was too late also indicated an inability to make good investment choices. So his parents had strongly suggested he attend the wedding, with an appropriate date on his arm.

All Marcus had to do was pick a woman.

"The options are limited and time is running short, Mr. Warren," Liberty said. She jammed her hands on her hips. "The wedding is in two weeks."

"Fine. I'll take you."

The effect of this statement was immediate. Liberty's eyes went wide and her mouth dropped open and her gaze dropped over his body. Something that looked a hell of a lot like desire flashed over her face.

Then it was gone. She straightened and did her best to look imperial. "Mr. Warren, be serious."

"I am serious. I trust you." He took a step toward her. "Sometimes I think…you're the only person who's honest with me. I want to take you to the wedding."

It was hard to say if she blushed, as she was already red-faced from their morning run and the heat. But something in her expression changed. "No," she said flatly. Before he could take the rejection personally, she added, "I—it—would be bad for you."

He could hear the pain in her voice. He took another step toward her and put a hand on her shoulder. She looked up, her eyes wide and—hopeful? His hand drifted from her shoulder to her cheek and damned if she didn't lean into his touch. "How could you be bad for me?"

The moment the words left his mouth, he realized he'd pushed this too far.

She shut down. She stepped away and turned to face the lake. "We need to head back to the office."

That's when he heard a noise. Marcus looked around, trying to find the source. A shoe box on the ground next to a trash can moved.

Marcus's stomach fell in. Oh, no—who would throw away a kitten? He hurried over to the box and pulled the lid off and—

Sweet Jesus. Not a kitten.

A baby.

Don't miss
HIS FOREVER FAMILY by Sarah M. Anderson
available February 2016 wherever
Harlequin® Desire books and ebooks are sold.

www.Harlequin.com